Happy Deathday To You

Milly Reynolds

ISBN: 1500275220
ISBN-13: 978-1500275228

DEDICATION

To my family.
Your continued support means the world to me.

Prologue

Florrie watched him as he put the finishing touches to the cake. He was calling something out to her, and even though she couldn't quite hear him, she recognised kindness in his voice. It was the flame that surprised her! She became quite frightened when she saw the lighted match in his hand, but after she saw him blow it out, she relaxed again. Although he had his back to her, she guessed that he was smiling as he stood, hands on hips, admiring his handiwork. She watched him as, with great care, he picked up the cake, then turned and walked towards her. Why was he singing 'Happy Birthday'? It wasn't her birthday! Still singing, he put the cake down in front of her and as she looked at the flickering flames on the candles, Florrie squealed.

One

I sat watching the second hand of the clock on the wall make its journey ever onwards. Time stops for no one, unless of course the battery runs down! The paperwork was finished and a pile of envelopes sat on the edge of my desk waiting expectantly for its descent into the darkness of the post-box. Local cats had been found and returned to their grateful owners and all the little old ladies of the town had been helped across the road. A good day's work! Now all I had to look forward to was … badminton! A brand new sports bag crouched in the corner of the room, mocking me. Why, oh why had I agreed to join Simon for a game of badminton?

Simon Leavesly was the local solicitor; he had never married and was a man of my own age. Over the past few months we had become quite friendly, often meeting for the occasional drink after work to discuss the finer things in life – mainly beer and sport. Then, one fateful day, Simon had decided that he needed to get fitter, so he had suggested that instead of staring into the bottom of a beer glass – something I enjoy doing – we should run around a badminton court! I had said, 'yes'! The word had made a run for it before I'd had the chance to close my mouth and it had announced itself in Simon's ear. He had positively beamed. Now, the first game was to be this evening, unless a major crime should suddenly require my urgent attention. I crossed my fingers.

"Shepherd!"

Alan Shepherd bounded into my office. The awful

events of a few months ago had left their mark upon him. A sadness now lurked in the corner of his eyes, a sadness which, funnily enough, always disappeared whenever Cat Browning entered a room. She, like Shepherd, had been an unwilling pawn in that same chess game. However, it had changed her life for the better. She no longer worked for Bob Archer at The Cat and Fiddle, something which pleased me greatly. Archer was a nasty piece of work, of that I was sure. I couldn't put my finger on it but whenever he entered the bar, I would see shadows rush to hide, which told me that some day in the future I would have the pleasurable task of snapping handcuffs around his fat little wrists. Cat's decision to work for Simon Leavesly had definitely been the right one. On top of that it had also meant that she was no longer renting Archer's grotty little cottage. In fact, she now lived at Elderton Manor with Shepherd, as his lodger. It was a good arrangement for both of them and I had high hopes of this 'business' relationship developing into something more meaningful.

"Anything needing my attention, lad?"

Shepherd sat himself in the chair opposite me and smiled mischievously.

"Nothing at all, Sir. You go and enjoy your game."

"Hmm!" I could see that he was enjoying himself.

"You can hang onto my racket for a while if you want, Sir. I don't really play anymore, I need something more … energetic." The stifled laughter escaped. "The paramedics have been alerted, I suppose?"

"Are you suggesting that I am not in peak physical fitness, lad?"

"Well, you're not quite as nimble as you were, Sir, are you? Look how you fell over when you came to my aid at Tony Wood's farm."

"It was dark!"

"It was the afternoon."

"The rakes were hidden in the grass."

"Well, you be careful, Sir." Shepherd stood and struck a perfect serve with his invisible racket. "After all, a man of your age needs to take things easy." He winked and was in the safety of the corridor before I had a chance to pick up a pen to throw after him. Damn! My reactions would need to be a lot sharper tonight.

At six-thirty I was looking in the changing room mirror at my white knees which were peeping out with some embarrassment from my white shorts; my white t-shirt was stretched tightly over my stomach. In fact, everything about me was white, except for my face which was a delicate cherry pink. Bending to tie my trainers had really taken it out of me!

"Ready, Mike?" Simon Leavesly opened the door and peered in. "You OK? You seem a bit flushed."

"I'm fine! It's just a bit warm in here."

I picked up my racket and followed Simon out into the corridor. He was about three inches taller than me but of a more athletic build. His white t-shirt was baggy! As my footsteps padded along towards the badminton courts, I knew exactly what a condemned man must have felt like on his way to the gallows. This was it! No escape!

"Sir! Glad to have caught you."

Shepherd's voice echoed in the enclosed space and I turned around to give him a piece of my mind. How dare he invite himself along to watch my humiliation! The look on his face, however, stopped me in my tracks and the reprimand stuck in my throat.

"You're needed, Sir. Now!"

"Simon, we'll make it another time." I shook Simon's hand and retraced my steps to the car-park with Shepherd in pursuit.

"Well, lad? What is it?"

"A birthday cake, Sir. A birthday cake and an over-fed pig."

Two

As we drove to Harold Chamber's farm, I was still trying to decide why a pig with a birthday cake should need a visit from the police. What was the crime? Can pigs even commit crimes?

Harold was in the farmyard as we pulled up, watching for our arrival. The smoke from his pipe was curling around his head like a white woolly hat, waiting to watch events unfold.

I opened the door of my green Mondeo and extended my hand. As I registered the shock on Harold Chamber's face, I realised with some horror that I was still in my brilliantly white t-shirt and shorts. I had been so grateful that a case had materialised to whisk me away from the badminton court of hell that I had forgotten to change. My clothes, and my trusty notebook, were still in the changing room locker. Damn! I saw Harold's gaze taking in my white legs and, as his eyes travelled upwards, I crossed my arms across my stomach to protect it from ridicule.

"Sorry to have interrupted your whatever it was, Mr Malone, but there's something odd in the pig-sty. I thought you'd be just the chap to sort this out."

"I'll do my best, Mr Chambers. Lead on!"

At that moment, Shepherd leapt from beside the car to appear at my shoulder.

"Sir, it's a farm!" he whispered.

"Well done, lad. You'll make an inspector yet."

"Your white trainers, Sir. You're going to a pig-sty."

The penny dropped, followed by some fifty pence pieces and a bundle of notes. He was right! My brand new white trainers would be ruined.

"Be with you in a moment, Mr Chambers," I called out to the retreating figure. He turned around, perplexed.

Hurrying to the rear of my car, I unlocked the boot to see what I could find to put on my feet. I pushed aside newspapers, a football and some bags. Shepherd came to assist in the search and he immediately found a kettle which he held out in some amazement.

"A kettle, Sir?"

"A long and steamy story – I'll tell you one day."

"No shoes, Sir."

I stared down at my sparkling white trainers. The thought of cleaning them after a trip to a pig-sty was almost too much to bear and I sighed.

"Plastic bags, Sir. Tie the bags around your feet."

My down-turned face did a flip and I beamed happily at him.

"Brilliant! Just brilliant!"

Minutes later, with one foot in a white and blue Tesco bag and the other in a green M&S bag, I crinkled my way over the yard to join Harold Chambers who, drawing heavily on his pipe, had a look of utter bewilderment on his face as he took in my snazzy new footwear. Without uttering a single syllable, he turned once more towards the sty.

Florrie, the accused sow, was lying on her side and feeling rather sorry for herself at the back of the sty when we arrived; a pool of vomit lay beside her.

She refused to look at Harold as he opened the door to the enclosure. The first thing that I noticed was a paper plate decorated with balloons and several broken pink candles; a ripped party hat was in the far corner. As for the cake, yellow crumbs were scattered all over the mud and a lump of cream was balancing precariously on Florrie's snout.

"This is just as I found it, Mr Malone. I don't know where the cake came from. I know old Florrie wouldn't have stolen it – she's a good lass, that she is."

"Is it by any chance her birthday? Could someone have given her a cake as a present?"

"Florrie's birthday is in November. Everybody knows that!" Harold was quite indignant. "Everybody local, that is."

I decided to give him a minute to calm down and nodded to Shepherd.

"Have a look around, lad."

Shepherd threw me a look that told me that the last thing he wanted to do was get on his hands and knees in a pig-sty. I smiled encouragingly at him. After all, I had great faith in him; Shepherd could sniff out a clue as surely as a pig could sniff out a truffle. Taking a step back towards the wall where the dry mud was, I watched him take a deep breath and plunge his hands into the mud.

"What time did you last check on Florrie, Mr Chambers?"

"I gave her some feed before I had my tea at five."

"And the sty was OK then?"

He nodded.

"And you heard no one in the yard?"

"Not a thing. The wife didn't either. I came out to lock up and found all this." He waved his arm across the sty in despair.

"Was Florrie wearing the party hat when you came to lock up?"

"Don't be daft, man! How can a pig put a hat on? It was in the corner and the cake was in bits – what was left of it. She's got a sore tummy now after eating all that. Look at her – that's was pigging out does to you."

I turned away from him partly to conceal a smile and partly to see what eating a whole birthday cake does to a pig. Florrie was certainly feeling very sorry for herself – she had now settled herself down in the corner with her head under her trotters and her back to us.

Shepherd stood and came over to me.

"Nothing out of the ordinary, Sir. Cake crumbs, broken pink candles which appear to have been lit, a torn party hat and a few rose petals."

I looked down at his muddy trousers and wondered what on earth I could put on my car seat to protect it.

"Well, Mr Malone?" Harold Chambers interrupted my dreams of plastic covered car seats.

"I'm not sure what it is you want me to do, Mr Chambers." I was very calm and I hoped comforting. "After all no crime has been committed."

"No crime! Of course there's been a crime!" he spluttered. "Someone has fed a birthday cake to my pig. I won't have it, I tell you. I want him caught and put behind bars."

"I'll see what I can do."

With Shepherd at my side, we said our good-byes and squelched and crinkled our way back to the car.

"Did you take any photos, lad?"

"Yes, Sir."

"We'll keep them just in case this is the start of a crime-wave."

"Or the start of a birthday party, Sir."

I decided to ignore Shepherd's attempt at humour. I had more important things on my mind. What was I going to do about my car seats?

Three

*Taking the packet from the kitchen drawer, he
counted eight pink candles out onto the worktop.
After placing them carefully onto the freshly
decorated cake, he stood back to admire his work.
Perfect! He retrieved a cake tin from the top of the
fridge and packed the cake away, taking great care
not to crush the candles. Satisfied, he collected his
car keys and left the kitchen with the tin hidden
underneath his jacket.*

The afternoon sun was streaming through the
office window and unable to resist, I created a little
shadow play of 'The Three Pigs' on my blotter. My
fingers entwined to create elaborate houses of straw
and wood, and pigs ran happily from one side of my
desk to the other. However, before the house of
bricks could be built, Shepherd bounded through the
door.

"Sir, Martin Webb has just phoned. He has found
a squashed birthday cake in his pig-sty."

"Another one?" My hands unclasped themselves
and the Big Bad Wolf trotted off to find a pig
stuffed with cake.

"Was it the pig's birthday?"

"No, Sir."

"In that case, we'd better investigate. Come on,
lad."

Martin Webb's farm reminded me of the toy farm
that I used to play with when I was a lad; the barns
and the farmhouse were tiny and neat, and the

animals were immaculately turned out and silent. Martin was in the yard when we arrived, surrounded by several chickens who were all busily pecking his boots. As the sun shone on their brown feathers, I thought of the rich, brown chocolate chickens that I devoured every Easter. I licked my lips and imagined all that creamy chocolate sliding down my throat. Heaven!

A sharp peck on my ankle brought me back to reality.

"Mr Webb, I'm D. I. Malone." I extended my hand and a firm hand grasped mine and shook it firmly. I looked up into Martin Webb's face which was wrinkled and jolly and I immediately warmed to him.

"I feel a bit silly for calling you out like this, but I was so surprised to see a birthday cake in the sty with Sadie." He smiled apologetically.

"No problem at all. In fact, this is the second birthday cake that has been found in two days."

"Really!"

"Lead the way, please."

Even though I had arrived fully prepared, dressed in rubber trousers and wellies, this farmyard was spotless; I could have worn pure white fur slippers it was so clean. In the pig-sty, Sadie was lying on her side and looking rather green; she had recently been sick. Considering that there were very few crumbs to be seen, I quickly guessed why she was feeling so poorly. This little piggy had not only been to market, she had eaten all the cakes. I nodded to Shepherd who looked around the gleaming sty and dropped to his knees, quite happy that he would not end up covered in mud today.

"Well, lad?"

"Pink candles, Sir. There are lots of bits so it's a bit difficult to see how many there were."

"Anything else?"

"The remains of a green party hat, a little piece of pink icing and some rose petals. Look's like it was a birthday cake for a girl."

I made several notes in my notebook, noticing as I did so that this crime scene was identical to the scene at Harold Chambers' farm. I closed the book with that satisfying snap that I always enjoy. Shepherd was still looking around.

"There are no signs of any footprints, Sir. In fact, no sign of anything at all."

"Ok, thanks." I turned to Martin Webb. "Did you notice anything strange?"

He rubbed his chin thoughtfully, and thinking back to my shadow play of earlier in the day, I half expected him to repeat the Big, Bad Wolf's catchphrase. "Nothing at all, Mr Malone. After lunch I went down the field in the tractor."

"Did you see anyone?"

"There are always cars going up and down the lane. I never noticed anyone stop."

"What time did you come back to the yard?"

"Around three. Sorry, I'm not being very helpful, am I?"

"Don't worry about it."

Nodding to Shepherd, we made our way back to the car.

"Sounds like the beginning of a crime wave, lad. But, what the crime is, I haven't quite decided yet."

"Does this mean….?" he stopped, quivering with anticipation.

"It does, lad. It does. We need to get the crime-board up from the basement."

Two hours later and the crime-board had once again been installed in my office. After it had been banished to the basement a few months ago following the resolution of the Black murder case, I had hoped never to see it again, but now here it was. In the centre were photographs not only of the two pigs but also of the remains of the two cakes. As I stood back to try to find the link between these two senseless crimes, Shepherd arrived with a mug a tea which he placed in front of me.

"No biscuits, lad?"

He grinned. "I didn't want to spoil your fitness regime, Sir."

"A walk onto a badminton court hardly constitutes a fitness regime," I growled. "I'll have a custard cream."

Shepherd disappeared and within seconds he was back with not one, but two custard creams. Ah, life's small pleasures!

By five o'clock I was still no closer to solving the mystery of the birthday cakes. Who buys birthday cakes for pigs? With a sigh, I closed my desk drawer and locked it.

"Shepherd!"

Alan Shepherd bounced into the office.

"I'm going home, lad. Ring me immediately if there are any developments."

"Yes, Sir. You haven't forgotten that you are having a drink with Cat and I tonight, have you?"

"No, I'll be there."

Locking the office door behind me, I set out for the relative peace and tranquillity of my little cottage.

Four

Ophelia was sitting in her basket, glaring at me. No amount of tit-bits and treats would appease her. It was her fourth birthday and I had forgotten to present her with her traditional gift. No birthday cakes for my feline mistress, she demanded only the best smoked salmon for her special day and I had forgotten. I was in the dog house!

I decided to take my mug of tea into the lounge and put my feet up for an hour before I met Shepherd and Cat. Although Shepherd always insisted that the two of them were just friends, just lodgers, I had my suspicions. In my opinion they were soul mates and I had high hopes of being able to buy a new hat in the very near future. I envied them their youth and their hope; I had lost mine on that dreadful day five years ago. I missed having someone to talk to when I came home in the evenings, I missed having someone to hold, someone to … The ringing of the phone awakened me from my trip down memory lane.

"Malone."

"Mike, it's Simon."

I groaned. "Simon, nice to hear from you. Sorry about last night."

"No problem at all. Anyway, I've rebooked the court for tomorrow night. Seven o'clock. Are you free?"

I scratched my head. Should I make up an excuse, or should I just get it over with? Heads or tails? I flipped an imaginary coin, watched it twirl in the air and come to land on my outstretched hand. Heads!

"Seven is fine, Simon. Shall I meet you there?"

"Super job. Martin and Richard are going to join us."

"Sorry?"

"You must know them, Mike. Martin Goddard is an accountant with Baker Goddard and Richard Austin is manager of National Providence Building Society."

"I know who they are, Simon." I tried to keep the irritation from my voice. Richard and I had become friends when I first moved into the town and sorted out my bank accounts. I had even helped him to teach his eldest daughter to drive. "I'm just wondering why they are joining us."

"Doubles, Mike. See you tomorrow."

I was left staring at the receiver in a state of shock. I couldn't believe it! My first game of badminton in over twenty years was going to be a doubles game. I could see it now. The story of my humiliation would keep this town amused for years. It would even become one of the town's ancient legends!

My mood had not improved by the time that I entered The King's Head. This was one of the better public houses, a vast improvement upon The Cat and Fiddle; there was always a friendly welcome from Frank Bassett, the landlord, who was the complete opposite of Bob Archer. Frank was the product of many hours in the gym; his toned muscles always made me feel as if I was a jelly on legs. On the other hand, Bob Archer was the product of too much of his own beer and he definitely was a walking jelly.

Cat and Shepherd were in the corner, deep in conversation. As I hadn't been spotted, I took the opportunity to observe them as I got my drink. Cat's red hair shone in the warm lighting of the pub. She was leaning close to Shepherd to hear what he was saying; the buzz from the bar was quite loud. As I watched, he lightly touched her wrist and a gentle blush appeared on her cheek. Yes, this pair were definitely *just* good friends!

Picking up my pint, I made my way over to them.

"Sir, you're on time!"

"I'm always on time."

"Hello, Mike." Cat leaned over and kissed my cheek. "Are you all ready for tomorrow? I heard Simon on the phone to you as I was leaving."

Shepherd raised his eyebrows inquisitively and I addressed my reply to him.

"Simon has rebooked the badminton court."

A twinkle appeared in his eye.

"That's good, Sir."

"No! No it is not! He's arranged a game of doubles!"

Shepherd had been taking a sip of orange juice as I was speaking and he snorted into it as Laughter ran up and tapped him on the shoulder. Tears came to his eyes as he coughed and spluttered into his glass.

"That's brilliant, Sir! That's priceless!"

"I'm glad that you find it so funny."

Cat put her hand on mine. "You'll enjoy it, Mike. It'll also do you good to get a bit of exercise. After all, it can't be good for you sitting around everyday."

"If you both don't mind, I'd like to change the topic of conversation. I came out to relax, not to be ridiculed and lectured about my standard of fitness."

Cat and Shepherd exchanged a glance and with huge smiles across their faces, they talked enthusiastically about their plans to go on a sight-seeing trip to London.

Five

The church clock chimed the quarter hour. Quarter to eight. He sighed. She normally left at half-past seven on the dot. At half-past seven he had been ready and waiting. Now, his legs were stiff and the inside windows were beginning to steam up from the heat of his body. This was hopeless! He would have to come back tomorrow. As he stretched out one leg slowly, trying to urge the blood back into his toes, he heard the front door open. Raising himself slightly, he saw Suzanne Lloyd step into the warm morning air and heard her shout 'good-bye' to her family. He quickly ducked down again and covered himself with the car rug. Her footsteps were getting closer. Would she notice the steamed-up windows? If she raised the alarm, he would never be able to make a dash for it. He heard the key in the lock and the mechanism click loudly; the open door let in a rush of welcome fresh air. There was a dull thud as she threw her bag onto the passenger seat and the creak of the springs as she settled herself into the driving seat. The car door closed.

He reacted with a speed that even surprised him. Rising like a cobra from a basket, he put his left hand across her mouth while his right stroked her throat with the knife that it had firmly in its grasp. In the rear view mirror he saw her eyes widen in recognition and shock. Her hand flew to her throat but it was too late. Her blood had been spilt and he watched it gathering in a glistening pool at her feet, staining forever her silver grey shoes. As he looked once more into the rear view mirror, he saw the light leave her eyes.

Silently, he opened the rear door and rolled into the protective shade of the hedge. Keeping his body close to the ground, he followed the hedge round to the back of the house where the gate that he had forced earlier was still open. He slipped through it and retrieved his bike from under the hedgerow. One minute later and he was camouflaged by the early morning stampede to work.

The next morning, Grayson waved me over to the desk as soon as I set foot in the station. He was holding the telephone receiver tight against his ear, and was scribbling away on his notepad. I waited.

"A murder!" he gasped.

The words ricocheted around the station and instantly Shepherd was by my side.

"Suzanne Lloyd, teacher at Northfields Primary. She has been found in her car with her throat cut."

I heard Shepherd's sharp intake of breath.

"Address, Grayson?"

"3 Primrose Hill."

Turning on my heels, I made for the station door, at the same time checking that my trusty notebook was in my pocket. Shepherd bounded after me with several plastic evidence bags in his grasp.

The ten minute drive to Primrose Hill had been in silence; murder was, thankfully, a rare event in this quiet little patch of Lincolnshire and as such, still had the power to shock. I had hoped that Shepherd could give me some background on Suzanne Lloyd, but unfortunately she was an unknown. He had been unable to provide me with any personal details whatsoever.

The house was at the end of a cul-de-sac and an ice blue Peugeot was standing outside the house on the drive. I noticed that every window in the house had its curtains pulled across as if it could not bear to witness this awful tragedy. The front door opened as we pulled up behind the Peugeot and a tall figure approached us. His shoulder length dark hair framed his ashen face; his eyes, full of confusion and distress, sought me out. As he came closer, he forced his eyes to hold mine, forced them not to look at the horror within his wife's car. I extended my hand and turned him back towards the house.

"Detective Inspector Mike Malone, Mr Lloyd. This is Detective Sergeant Alan Shepherd."

His hand was like a piece of soggy pastry, damp and lifeless. He opened his mouth to respond, but words had fled.

"You go back inside, Mr Lloyd. We'll deal with things out here. I'll pop in and talk to you presently."

He allowed me to guide him back to his own door. As he opened it, he suddenly turned, glanced quickly at the car and gripped my hand and arm. "Don't hurt her! Please don't hurt her!"

"We won't. Come on, let's get you inside."

I encouraged him to step inside the house and then closed the door firmly behind him. I turned back to Shepherd.

"Come on, lad. Let's see what we have here."

Suzanne Lloyd was still strapped in her car seat

like some grotesque waxwork figure. Her cream shirt was soaked with her blood and a pool had gathered at her feet; she looked as if she was paddling. Shepherd dropped to his hands and knees and looked around the car, searching for that one illusive clue that might set us on the right path.

"He must have been waiting for her in the car, Sir. There are no signs of a struggle or anything out here."

He opened the rear door of the car and clambered in.

"Anything?" I had my fingers crossed, hoping that the murderer might have been careless enough to leave a trace behind.

"Two dark hairs on the car rug, Sir. It looks as if he could have used it to hide himself."

"Jason Lloyd has dark hair."

"These are dark and wavy, Sir. Jason Lloyd's hair is long and straight. Suzanne is blond."

"What about the children?"

"Maybe, we'll know when we see them."

"Let's hope the kids are blond or ginger. Good spot, lad. Bag them for evidence. Anything else?"

"She has some rose petals and a handkerchief in her pocket."

"That's odd, I wonder why. Bag them just in case. Anything else?"

"Nothing, Sir."

Shepherd clambered out as the sound of sirens drifted towards us on the breeze. The team were on their way. I left Shepherd on his knees examining the drive and went to find Jason Lloyd.

An hour later we were on our way back to the station. Lloyd had been able to tell us nothing! He had been busy in the kitchen preparing the day's packed lunches, lunches that would now be uneaten, when Suzanne had left for work. It was only when he didn't hear the car start that he went outside to check that everything was alright. He had seen nothing.

Shepherd's fingertip search had been more successful. Broken twigs at the bottom of the hedge running around the house to the rear gate suggested that the murderer had crept along the hedge to avoid being seen from the house. The fact that the rear gate had also been forced showed that this had been his point of entry, and exit. As for gaining access to the car, Lloyd had told us that he was constantly moaning at Suzanne because of her tendency to leave it unlocked on the drive. However, that was where our investigation ended. The lane running along the back of the house was sheltered from view and no other properties overlooked it. In one direction it was a nice walk to the next village; in the opposite direction, it joined the main road which was always extremely busy. I had as much chance of finding a witness who saw someone in the lane as I had of winning my badminton game tonight. The path was also regularly used by couples, children and fitness fanatics, so finding footprints was also going to be impossible. It was a dead end.

Back at the station, my first job was to clear the crime-board of the pictures of pigs and birthday cakes. That little crime wave had now paled into insignificance. This dreadful murder had to take priority. As I placed the last photograph in my desk drawer, Shepherd arrived with a mug of tea.

"No biscuits?"

"Think of tonight's game, Sir," he grinned. "You don't want biscuits to slow you up, do you?"

"I am thinking very carefully about tonight's game. Two custard creams, lad. Now!"

He scampered out of the office and returned with two biscuits as requested. I looked at them with longing, but decided to complete the crime-board first. Photographs of Suzanne and Jason Lloyd, their family, their house and the blue Peugeot were sitting in a pile on my desk, embarrassed to be at the centre of so much attention. Under Shepherd's watchful gaze, I carefully arranged them on the board, with Suzanne Lloyd in the centre. Once the last drawing pin had been pushed into place, I turned away. I could feel the eyes of the family following me, pleading with me to catch the person who had destroyed their happiness.

Picking up my tea, I took a sip, at the same time pushing the biscuits over to Shepherd. I had lost my appetite.

By five o'clock the investigation had ground to a halt; door to door enquires had turned up no leads. At Northfields Primary, Suzanne Lloyd's colleagues neither knew of anyone with a grudge against her nor could they think of anyone who had been particularly aggressive towards her. I had no leads except for two dark wavy hairs. I was on a roundabout with no exits.

Shepherd knocked and poked his head around the door. "I'm off, Sir. Enjoy your game."

"Good night, lad."

I listened to his footsteps disappear down the corridor and after locking the hairs securely in my drawer, I set off for my appointment at the badminton court.

Six

He packed the car and returned to the kitchen. The birthday cake was in the centre of the table; the pink icing was highlighted by pure white frosting. Taking a tin down from the top shelf, he placed the cake into it with the utmost care. That task completed, he opened a drawer and counted out eight pink candles which he dropped into his pocket. With the tin nestling against his body, he left the kitchen. He left the house.

Once again my face was a cherry pink from the exertion of bending down to tie my trainers. Picking up my racket, I quickly turned my back on the changing-room mirror; I could feel my t-shirt complaining, I didn't want to watch it as it fought to keep my stomach covered. With two practice swings perfectly executed, I made my way to the court where the other three were already gathered.

"Mike! Shall we see if we can actually start a game tonight?" Simon was in a particularly cheerful mood.

As I shook hands with Richard, I noticed with some small pleasure that his t-shirt was engaged in a battle as fierce as my own. However, his t-shirt was on the losing side as expanses of pink, dimpled flesh kept escaping from its grasp.

"Good to see you, Mike. I didn't know you played, you kept that quiet." His hand-shake was, as usual, that of a dominant male. With a sinking heart I realised that Richard was also going to be the type of player who always had to win.

"I don't," I laughed. "My ideal sport, as you should know, involves lifting a beer glass, but Simon persuaded me that this would be a good idea."

"Judging by your tum, Mike, I think it's an excellent idea." Martin Goddard prodded my stomach playfully with the end of his racket and I resisted the temptation to stick the end of my racket somewhere else!

Martin Goddard was everything that I despised; tall and athletic with a six-pack rippling under his skin-tight t-shirt.

"At your age, Mike, you need to keep the podge down, you know. A little gentle exercise everyday, that's what you need. Look at me – a 5 mile run everyday without fail and I never use a car unless I have to." Martin slapped me on the back in a spirit of camaraderie.

"I think I'll just grow old gracefully, thank you." The words pushed themselves out through my clenched jaw and I kept my hands firmly by my side just in case they decided to slap Martin on the back, or in the stomach, or in the face. "Shall we play?"

I plodded on to the court and left the three athletes to decide my fate.

Simon's game plan was, in my opinion, a stroke of genius. I stood at the net ready to hit a smash while Simon ran around missing shot after shot after shot. I'd forgotten how much fun sport could actually be! After losing the first game heavily, Simon called me over for a team meeting. He was panting like an overweight, overheated dog and his white t-shirt was soaked with sweat.

"In the next game, Mike, try coming back sometimes to support. We can't rely on just the smash shot, we need to try to pick up some of the other points."

I nodded in agreement and we returned to the court to await Martin's serve. Simon returned it and Martin lobbed it back. The shuttlecock was in the air! I watched it reach its summit and then begin its descent. I raised my racket. I was perfectly poised to receive and return it. I drew back my arm and…

Seven

He had been sitting in the farmyard for two hours waiting for the lights to go out, and now his joints had seized. He had arrived too early! It would have been more sensible to have gone home first, watched a bit of mind-numbing TV, and then have driven out here. But he had been eager, excited.

As the last light went out, he opened the car door and painfully stretched out his legs before heading to the pig-sty. The pig was sleeping; its gentle snufflings amused him, but they did not extinguish the desire within him. Clambering over the gate, he unpacked the cake and placed it on the floor of the sty next to the trough. That done, he searched in his pocket and found the candles which he carefully arranged on the cake. A sudden noise behind him caused him to look around, straight into the eyes of a very large sow that was clearly not happy to have been awoken. Before he had a chance to move, she had charged and he now found himself face-down in the cake with a candle up his nose. Ruined! He had not even had the chance to sing 'Happy Birthday'.

I opened my eyes expecting to see the green walls of the sports centre. Instead I saw only white. I closed them quickly. Where was I? What had happened? I slowly opened one eye. Everything was still white but also, eerily silent. I was dead! I had had a heart attack! Exercise had killed me! I closed my eye again and waited for the choirs of angels.

"Mr Malone?"

A woman's voice. An angel come to guide me. I

opened my eyes and found myself looking into the creased face of a heavily overweight woman who was bending over me. Her tight greying curls hung around her face like shabby, unwashed curtains; her smile was lop-sided and revealed yellow, uneven teeth. And, she had been eating onions! I shut my eyes and screamed. I was in Hell!

"Mr Malone! Calm down!" I felt a firm hand on my arm. "Calm down! You're in hospital."

I opened my eyes again, slowly. The face was still there, but thankfully not as close.

"You've had an accident, Mr Malone. You've had nasty crack on the head that needed several stitches and you have a cut above your eye that also needed some stitching. How do you feel?"

I opened my mouth but words refused to appear, so I nodded and immediately wished that I hadn't. My head felt as if a brass band was inside it, marching in industrial boots. I raised my hand and instead of hair, found only a coarse crepe bandage. The nurse patted my arm.

"Your friend's waiting outside to take you home. I'll tell him to come in."

I closed my eyes again and heard her footsteps fade into the distance.

Thoughts were running about inside my head, running around the feet of the marching bandsmen. I tried to capture them, to hold onto them. How had I ended up in hospital – with stitches? Had the badminton court been invaded by hoodies from the estate? Had we been attacked by badminton purists who couldn't stand to see their precious game abused for a moment longer? Where were the others? Had they been hurt as well or was I the only unfortunate victim? Before I could pin a fluttering thought to the wall, I heard more footsteps approach my bed.

"Mike? How are you feeling?" I opened my eyes and saw Simon's concerned face looking down on me. "You gave us all a right turn!"

"What happened?" My voice had returned.

"Don't you remember? No, you probably wouldn't, would you? We both went for the same shot and I'm afraid I hit you with my racket. You stumbled and your head connected with the metal foot of the badminton net. We thought you were a goner, there was so much blood. The centre had to close the courts down – they were not happy."

"Where's my stuff?"

"In my car. Your car is still at the sports centre, but I've got your keys. You can pick it up in the morning. Now let's get you home. I rang Alan Shepherd and he is going to crash at yours tonight to keep an eye on you. Head injuries and all that, you know."

"I'll be fine"

"No arguments, it's Dr's orders. Now then, let's try and get you out of this bed."

Eight

I hadn't heard the alarm, but I had heard the footsteps approaching. I opened my eyes and Shepherd was standing next to the bed, a mug of tea in his hand.

"How are you feeling, Sir?"

"Head's sore, but otherwise OK."

I shuffled up the bed, took the tea and sipped it gratefully. My mouth was like the Sahara Desert.

"We may as well travel to the station together, lad." I started to swing my legs to the side of the bed.

"You need the day off, Sir. You've had a nasty fall."

"Rubbish! We have a murder to solve."

His face showed disapproval, but as he wasn't my mother, there wasn't a lot he could do. I was big enough and ugly enough to take care of myself.

The drive to the station was quiet, unnaturally quiet. I was aware of Shepherd glancing nervously in my direction. Something was on his mind.

"Spit it out, lad."

"What, Sir?"

"Whatever it is that's worrying you. What is it?"

"You, Sir."

"I'm touched, lad." I winked at him. "I didn't know you cared."

"I don't … I mean I do … Oh!"

"Just spit it out, lad."

"Do you remember anything about last night, Sir?"

"No! I was asleep."

"No, you weren't, Sir. You woke up, you were sobbing."

I kept my eyes on the road ahead. Not again! I thought the nightmares were a thing of the past.

"You were sobbing, Sir. You kept repeating the name David over and over again." I could feel his eyes on me but I refused to look at him. The bang on the head had evidently opened a door that had been closed for a long while. What other locked doors had it opened? What other memories were going to steal up on me when I was least expecting them? "I tried consoling you, Sir, but you would have none of it. It was awful."

I concentrated on the number plate of the car ahead. What could I say to him?

"It was just a nightmare, lad. Nothing more. Sorry I woke you."

From the corner of my eye I could still see anxiety in his eyes.

"Are you sure you're OK, Sir?"

"I'm fine! Fine! After that game of badminton I was bound to have a bad dream, wasn't I?" I laughed but it echoed hollowly around the car.

My morning coffee was still standing on my desk with the steam rising ever upwards when Shepherd bounded into the office.

"Fred Greengrass has found a birthday cake, Sir."

I groaned. I had a murder to solve; a murder with no leads. I didn't have time to chase around the countryside looking for someone who thought it was funny to give birthday cakes to pigs.

"I'm getting fed up with this little game. When I catch this cake-loving joker I'm going to throw the book at him for wasting police time and resources."

I looked sadly at the coffee that was destined to go cold and got to my feet. "We'd better have a look, I suppose. Remember to grab your wellies, lad."

Fred and Betty Greengrass were in their garden when we arrived. Emily had now grown a lovely woolly coat and she smiled shyly at me as I opened the gate. I patted her head. It was funny how I had grown to have quite a soft spot for sheep.

"Morning, Fred. Morning, Betty."

"Morning, Mr Malone." Fred nodded to Shepherd. "Funny business this is, Mr Malone. To be honest I did think that Harold was having me on the other night in the pub when he was telling us all about his Florrie. But, damn me, if it don't go and happen to me too! In my very own pig-sty!"

"Let's go, shall we?"

Shepherd and I had already put our wellies on, so we were able to stomp quite happily across the yard after Fred.

"You'll need to watch your back when you go into the sty, Mr Malone. Our Bertha can be a bit unfriendly at times."

I didn't look at Shepherd, but I heard him groan.

When we got to the sty, Bertha was standing on guard and giving us the evil eye. Immediately, I noticed that things here were not quite the same. For one thing, the cake hadn't been eaten, just squashed. Secondly, the candles did not appear to have been lit. And thirdly, and most exciting of all, a little brown paper bag was on the floor beside the cake. Could this be a clue?

"In you go, lad." I slapped Shepherd on the back reassuringly.

"Will she bite me, Mr Greengrass?" he asked timidly.

Fred chuckled. "No, lad! If Bertha doesn't like you, she just knocks you over and tramples on you. She don't bite."

Shepherd did not look at all consoled, but, taking the bull by the horns, he clambered over the gate and I heard the squelch as his wellies disappeared into the mud. Bertha watched him.

"Good pig! Nice Bertha!" Shepherd called out soothingly.

Bertha snorted and I saw, with some amusement, Shepherd close his eyes and the colour fade from his pink cheeks. Bertha snorted again and trotted over to join him. Then, instead of charging him, she pushed her snout into his hand in greeting. As Shepherd opened his eyes, I heard him exhale. He patted Bertha gently on the top of her head and she trotted off to the back of the sty and lay down. As he dropped to his knees, I wasn't sure whether it was with relief, or whether he was just eager to start his search.

Fred, Bertha and I looked on as Shepherd prodded and poked in the soft mud. Finally he raised himself back onto two legs and came over to report his findings.

"Well, Sir, the cake doesn't appear to have been touched by Bertha."

"Bertha wouldn't have eaten that muck!" Fred

butted in. "She only likes good quality swill."

Shepherd glanced at Fred and then continued. "It looks as if whoever put the cake into the pig-sty, fell into it head-first."

"How?" I was at a loss.

"Because if he turned his back on Bertha, she would have charged him – sent him flying." Fred's face was rosy pink with delight. "Good old girl! Well done, Bertha!"

"The thing is, Sir," Shepherd was trying manfully to continue his report, "in the icing there is an impression of a pair of glasses. The man, or woman, doing this was wearing glasses when he landed in the cake."

"Don't suppose you can make out a type, can you?"

"Wire frame, Sir."

"Good work, lad."

"Not only that, Sir, he never had chance to light the candles. There are eight unlit candles in and around the cake."

"Brilliant!" Anything else?"

"A couple of dark hairs that got caught in the icing."

"What about a party hat?"

"Never had chance to use it, Sir. It is still folded up in the brown paper bag. There are also a handful of rose petals in there as well."

"Excellent! Bag everything and we'll get back to the station."

As Shepherd was brushing himself down, a thought popped into my head, took off its coat and sat down. Eight pink candles!

"Fred!" I turned back to Fred who was busy feeding Bertha. "How old is Bertha?"

"Nearly six."

The thought laughed at my stupidity and left my head as quickly as it had arrived. However, the number eight must be significant. How many candles had been left at the other two farms? "Do we still have all the bits of candle from the other two incidents, lad?"

"Yes, Sir."

"Good. I've got a job for you when we get back. What are you like at jigsaws?"

Back at the station, the post-mortem report on Suzanne Lloyd was waiting for me. After quickly scanning it, I learned nothing more than I already knew. She had died when her throat was cut. There were no fibres in her airways which suggested that the killer was wearing latex gloves when he put his hand over her mouth to stop her screaming. There was a dark navy fibre under her fingernail which must have come from her attacker's sleeve as she fought to get away. Unfortunately, it was a common one hundred percent polyester fibre as worn by over half the population of the UK.

Grayson knocked on the door and entered, squeezing his large frame into my small office space. All around me, I heard the furniture breathing in.

"The lads have been asking around Primrose Hill again, Sir. By half past seven the High Street was teeming with traffic heading towards Lincoln. No one remembers seeing anything out of the ordinary, except for Mrs Chesterton from Number Twelve. She does remember seeing a man with a bike acting suspiciously at the top of the lane at about seven o'clock when she was on her way to buy her Woman's Weekly magazine. She noticed him because he was looking under the hedge as if he had lost something."

"Seven o'clock. What time was the murder called in?"

"Around seven forty-five, Sir."

"It might have been him, I suppose. There was no evidence of a car in the lane so it is possible he could have used a bike."

"But he would have been covered in blood. Wouldn't he have been a bit conspicuous, Sir?"

"The fibre under Suzanne Lloyd's fingernail was a dark navy. Blood wouldn't have been noticeable on an item of clothing of that colour. And remember that he was in the back seat. He would have had very little blood on him at all."

"True."

"On top of that, who looks for someone fleeing a murder scene on a bike?"

Grayson nodded, evidently in awe of my wisdom.

"Get someone to pay Mrs Chesterton another visit and see if you can get a more detailed description of him and the bike."

"Will do, Sir."

He left the office and the furniture breathed out again. Getting up from my seat, I went over to the crime-board. A man on a bike? Was it possible? As the Lloyd family watched me from their position near the centre of the board, I realised that not only was I clutching at straws, I had plunged head-first into the whole bloody haystack.

As I walked into my cottage after work, I noticed with dismay that Ophelia did not come to greet me. Was she displeased with my lack of progress as well? As the afternoon had progressed, the only new information had been that Mrs Chesterton had thought that the man with the bike might have been wearing glasses. However, his dark blue helmet had partly obscured her view. He was wearing a dark jacket; it might have been blue, or black. Brilliant! So my murderer might, or might not, be a man on a bike. He might, or might not, wear glasses. He might, or might not, have been wearing a dark navy jacket. Maybe I should just put up a poster saying, 'Murderer Wanted. Please Apply,' and see who turned up.

"Ophelia! Oh no!"

As I had walked into my kitchen, my day had suddenly turned from grey to black, or in this case red. Spread across the kitchen floor were the bloody remains of what had once been a starling. It must have fallen down the chimney and Ophelia had thought that it was a gift from Heaven, just for her. Judging by the secret smile on her face, she had evidently enjoyed torturing the poor frightened bird to death.

The chimney! Soot!

As the bird fell it would have dislodged several years worth of soot, it would have acted like a sweeping brush. I took a deep breath and headed for the lounge leaving Ophelia innocently licking her

44

bloodstained paws.

Total devastation awaited me. There had indeed been a fall of soot. Its black tentacles had spread out from the stone hearth onto not only my rug, but also across my wooden floor; not only across the chimney surround, but also over the silver photo frames that were on the hearth. I cast my eyes over the rest of the lounge. Everywhere there were feathers, glossy black starling feathers, and shit. Bird shit trailed down the back of my sofa and over my favourite cushion. The leaded windows were also dotted with tiny red specks of blood where the starling had tried to break out to freedom. Pulling off my jacket and rolling up my sleeves, I sighed. This was going to take all night!

By nine o'clock everything was back to normal, except for my favourite cushion which looked vulnerable and naked without its cover. Ophelia was sitting in the window, watching me with her big sad eyes. For the previous three hours I had ignored her every demand for attention. Now that everything was clean again, I felt more inclined to forgive her. After all, she was only doing what all cats do, chase and kill birds; act on instinct. That was what separated men from animals. It was only men who planned a murder in cold blood. That was a purely human trait.

Nine

He opened the bedroom door. Crossing to the perfectly made-up bed, he sat on the edge and looked around. If he closed his eyes, he could still hear her breathing. She was always close to him here when he closed his eyes. In the cold light of day, the pain of her absence was unrelenting. His hand moved towards the pillow and rested on the soft pink pig. He buried his fingers in its soft fur and a single tear of loss rolled down his cheek. Pigs had been her passion. They had also been her death.

As soon as I opened my eyes, I heard a banging and crashing as all my thoughts clamoured for attention. This was not going to be a good day. I swung my legs out of the bed and my bare foot connected with the little fat body of a spider; I felt it go pop! This was definitely not going to be one of my better days. I lifted my foot and eight spindly legs hung from it. Using the wall to assist me, I hopped to the bathroom and the shower. The spider goo washed off easily and the last I saw of my little arachnid friend, was a mangled corpse disappearing down the plug-hole.

By half past seven I was on my way to the station, contemplating what lay ahead. I still had no leads for the Suzanne Lloyd murder; I was still no closer to discovering who was presenting birthday cakes to pigs.

Parking the car, I made my way to the station,

opened the door and fell crashing to the floor.

"Oh, Mr Malone! Are you alright, duck?" Nellie was on her knees, fussing over me. "Oh, you're bleeding, duck! If I'd known you were coming, I'd have moved my mop and bucket."

Sitting up carefully, I put a hand to my head. Blood ran through my fingers and onto my trousers. I had split my stitches.

"Sir, let me help you." Shepherd bounded over from the desk and helped me to my feet.

"Don't fuss, lad! Don't worry, Nellie. I should have looked where I was going."

"Let me run you to the surgery, Sir, and get you re-stitched."

Before I had the chance to protest, Shepherd had taken hold of my elbow and was propelling me back out of the station towards his car. I closed my eyes. The thoughts in my head were running around with clashing cymbals. Two disasters and it wasn't even eight o'clock. What on earth was going to happen next?

I sat back in the chair as she rested her fingers on my cheek. Her touch was so gentle and tender that I barely noticed the cut being re-stitched. I took a deep breath and my senses were caressed by her light, floral perfume. My bad day had miraculously become a magical day.

"All done!" Her voice was rich and warm like sweet hot chocolate.

"Thanks a lot, sorry to have been a nuisance. It was good of you to fit me in." I was a babbling idiot.

47

"Not at all, Mr Malone. We must look after our brave policemen, mustn't we?"

She smiled and sunlight filled the room. I looked into her shining clear blue eyes and dived right in.

"I had been expecting to see Dr. Foreman. Is he on holiday?" I needed to know if this apparition was going to vanish as quickly as it had appeared.

"He retired last month. It was a very quick decision as he needed to move to take care of his father. I'm his replacement."

Brilliant!

"I look forward to seeing you again then, Dr."

"But hopefully under less blood-stained circumstances."

She smiled and extended her hand. As I gently took it in mine, I noticed that her left hand wore no rings! This was like my best ever birthday times ten!

"Goodbye, Mr Malone. It was very nice to meet you."

Reluctantly, I let go of her hand and left the surgery to go and find Shepherd. As I got back into the car, I realised with horror that I had not even asked her name!

Arriving back at the station, Grayson was looking out for us.

"Another birthday cake, Sir. Jim Wallace has just phoned."

"Thanks, Grayson,"

"But this time, Sir, the pig is dead!"

As we pulled into the farmyard, I noticed the

silence. There was no birdsong and even the sheep were not softly bleating. It was as if they were all in mourning for one of their friends. I was puzzled. This was the fourth cake that had been delivered, but the first death. What had changed? Was the cake now chocolate instead of vanilla?

Jim came out to meet us, his arms hanging helplessly by his sides. I understood. The pig would have been like a family pet and its death would leave a big hole, especially if it was a big pig.

"Terribly sorry for your loss, Jim." I shook his hand which was as heavy as lead. "Can you tell me what happened?"

"No idea, Mr Malone. Rosie was right as rain last night."

"You said on the phone that there was a birthday cake?"

"Yes! Some idiot put a cake in the sty with her."

"Can you take us to her?"

Jim took us through the farmyard. As we passed the chickens, I noticed that they all had their heads bowed. Likewise with the sheep, whose heads were hanging sorrowfully over the wire fence? Evidently, Rosie had been a popular pig in the farmyard.

As we approached the sty, Jim stood aside to let us go ahead. I nodded to Shepherd.

"Have a good look around, lad. See if you can spot anything that is different about either the cake or the sty."

Shepherd opened the gate and immediately dropped to his hands and knees to commence his fingertip search. He was careful to avoid the pool of vomit that was beside Rosie's lifeless body; she was lying on her side and she looked very peaceful. Casting my own eye over the sty, I saw the remains of the cake in the corner. It was still a vanilla sponge. Once again I could see broken pink candles, crushed rose petals and a trampled party hat. Everything seemed the same so why was the pig dead?

I turned back to Jim who was still a few feet away from the sty. He didn't want to look.

"How old was Rosie, Jim?"

"Four."

"And she was in good health?"

"Full of life. Never had a day's illness." He was keeping his eyes firmly on his boots.

"Could the cake have upset her? I saw that she had been sick."

He shook his head sadly. "She always had a slice of cake on special occasions. It's never upset her before."

I was getting nowhere.

"Did you hear anything strange last night?"

"Nothing."

"What about Jenny?" I remembered the vital clue that Jenny had given us in our last murder case.

"Nothing. Poor Jenny! It was her that found Rosie. She went to give her some breakfast. Poor lass, it's really upset her."

A thought knocked on the side of my head and passed my mind a note. I
read it carefully.

"I'd like Dan Marshall to take a look at Rosie, if that's OK, Jim?"

"That's fine."

He turned and as he made his way back to the farmhouse, I turned back to Shepherd who was still on all fours in the middle of the sty.

"Anything, lad?"

"Nothing different, Sir."

"OK. Take the photos, bag the candles and hat and let's get back."

"Yes, Sir"

As I watched him reach for the plastic bags the same thought delivered another note. I read this one twice.

"Bag up some of the cake as well, lad?"

"The cake, Sir?"

"We have always assumed that the cake was harmless, after all the other pigs just had upset tummies. What if the cake is, in fact, poisoned?"

Admiration at my genius flowed from Shepherd's eyes to surround me and give me a hearty pat on the back.

"Excellent thinking, Sir! Can you pass me another plastic bag, please?"

As I was signing off the last memo after lunch, the phone rang. It was Dan Marshall and he had phoned to advise me that Rosie had died as the result of eating a large quantity of rat poison. My hunch had been right. I replaced the receiver thoughtfully.

"Shepherd!"

The door opened and Shepherd bounded in.

"Rosie was poisoned. Get onto the lab and get them to make the analysis of the cake a priority."

"Yes, Sir."

While I waited for him to return, I picked up my

51

pen and doodled away on my blotter. By the time he had made the phone call and returned, a huge plate of eggs, bacon and sausages was sitting in the centre of my blotter. In each of the sausages there was a pink candle.

"They'll get back to us by the end of the day, Sir."

"It looks as if I've been wrong about this all along, lad."

"Sir?"

"I had whoever was leaving the cakes for the pigs down as some sort of time-wasting village idiot. But, it looks as if the intention was actually to kill them."

"But he didn't kill the first three, Sir."

"Maybe he was experimenting with how much poison to put in the cake. Evidently there wasn't enough in the first three cakes to kill the pigs. Remember, the pigs had been sick. The poison could have affected them, but not killed them."

"Bertha wasn't sick."

"Bertha didn't eat any cake."

"Sorry, Sir. I forgot."

"I've asked Dan to check out Florrie and Sadie."

"So what do we do now, Sir?"

"Put the photos of the pigs back on the crime-board, of course."

Shepherd walked over to the board and studied the photos of the Lloyd case.

"Sir?"

"What is it, lad?" I turned to see his face tense with excitement.

"At the Lloyd's we found two dark hairs on the car rug. In Bertha's sty there were dark hairs in the icing. What if the hairs are from the same person?"

I was incredulous!

"Do you really think that the person who is poisoning pigs is the same person who butchered Suzanne Lloyd?"

"Think back to Black case, Sir." Shepherd's voice had dropped to a whisper.

I nodded silently. He was right, I had to consider it. Going over to my cupboard, I retrieved my precious microscope. As I placed it on the desk a sudden burst of sunlight caught it and made it seem otherworldly. We gazed in amazement at the glistening object before us.

"Now let's see if it can shed light on this mystery."

I retrieved both packets of hairs from my desk and held them up to the light. Shepherd could be right. To the naked eye the hairs seemed remarkably similar. With great care, I prepared a slide and placed a hair from the car rug at the top and a hair from the sty at the bottom. As I manoeuvred the slide into place I took a deep breath.

I was aware of Shepherd watching me closely as I lowered my eye to the scope. Like me, he too was holding his breath.

As the hairs came into sharp focus, I gasped. They were identical! The colour, the curl, the thickness – they were identical! I looked up.

"Well, Sir?"

"You were right, lad. Look for yourself. It's the same person."

I had to sit down. I was stunned. Questions rushed into my mind and ran around slamming doors and

53

opening drawers in their search for answers. Shepherd looked up from the microscope, pulled up a chair and sat down.

"What now, Sir?"

"We need to re-examine everything and try and find a link."

"Mrs Chesterton thought the man she saw was wearing glasses and there was an impression of glasses in the icing."

"Good."

"There is also another connection, Sir. Roses! Petals have been found in every pig-sty and petals were found.."

"In Suzanne Lloyd's pocket."

Silence fell on the office as we both sat trying to find other connections between all of these senseless crimes.

"Any ideas, lad?"

"None, Sir. Have you?"

"I don't know where to start. Birthday cakes, pink candles, rat poison, a dead pig and a dead teacher. This doesn't make sense. Let's put everything on the crime-board and have another look."

Ten

The mix was just right. Now he could go back and finish off the pigs that had escaped their fate. But first, there was someone he had to see.

The crime-board was complete; pictures from all four pig-sties had been added and although the red arrows were making some connections, they were not making the one that I wanted. Alone in the centre of the board was Suzanne Lloyd. I still had no idea why she had been killed, but I knew that the answer was somewhere on the board.

"Sir! I think I've finally managed to complete the jigsaw." Shepherd rushed into the office panting with excitement. His blond hair had fallen over his eyes and I watched him shake it back into place.

"Jigsaw, lad?" Memories flooded my mind, memories of wet afternoons when the two of us would be on the floor huddled over little wooden pieces. I remembered how David's hair used to flop into his eyes as he concentrated, trying to fit that last piece in to complete the picture. Only then, when it was finished, would he lift his head and smile at me, a big beaming smile filled with love, sunshine and life. I felt a hand close around my heart, crushing it painfully.

"Sir, are you OK?" Shepherd was bending over me, his eyes full of concern. "You're awfully pale, Sir."

"I'm fine, lad." I pushed the memory back behind the door; I would have to find a way of locking it again. "What did you say about jigsaws?"

"The candles from the pig-sties, Sir. I've been trying to fit them all together."

"And?"

"I'm pretty sure that there were eight candles in each cake."

"Well done, lad." He glowed under my praise. "So the number eight must have some significance."

I picked up some more arrows, fastened them to the crime board and joined Shepherd. We both looked at the board in wonder.

"Any ideas, Sir?"

I rubbed my chin.

"The birthday cakes all have eight candles so…" Shepherd raised his head and looked at me, waiting for my genius to wash over him. Unfortunately, today my genius was staying firmly in bed. "So I don't know."

Shepherd lowered his head in disappointment. "So what do we do, Sir?"

"Well, I'm going to the primary school. I need to find out more about Suzanne Lloyd and her pupils. I want you to find out who sells pink candles."

I patted him on the shoulder and left the office.

Sarah Harding clasped her hands in front of her on the desk. Her shoulder length grey hair fell forwards as she leaned towards me.

"I'm not sure what you are asking, Mr Malone."

"Neither am I, Mrs Harding," I admitted. "I'm looking for the proverbial needle in a haystack, or in this case a candle in a pig-sty."

She sat back in her chair to observe me as I swam around in circles in my muddy duck pond. I tried again.

"I know that the person who murdered Suzanne Lloyd is also trying to poison the town's pigs."

"You already told me that." She glanced at her watch.

"I know. I'm trying to find something that links two seemingly unrelated things. If I can find that, then I can find the killer."

"So, I'll ask you again. What exactly do you want from me?" She leaned forward again and I was whisked back to a time many years ago when I stood, in short trousers, in front of another headmistress. What is this strange power that certain women in authority seem to have over men? I sighed and tried to organise my ideas into coherent sentences. I felt that the 'window' that Mrs Harding had found for me was very soon going to be closing.

"Ok. I know this might sound like a crazy idea, but, the number eight is important to the killer. The poisoned birthday cakes all had eight candles on them."

"So, I'll ask again, Mr Malone, what …"

"I'm wondering if Suzanne Lloyd has ever had a bad relationship with a parent of an eight year old girl?"

The look on Sarah Harding's face was priceless. If I could have framed it I would have been able to make a fortune at Sotheby's. With those few words I had just confirmed her opinion of me. Exhibit A, one bumbling country copper who has as much chance of solving a serious crime as he has of winning a ploughing competition. She sat back and folded her arms.

"Suzanne Lloyd was a well loved and a highly respected teacher. She has never had any problems with her pupils, nor has she had any problems with their parents. I suggest you concentrate your efforts elsewhere and not in my school which is devastated by her death. Good day, Mr Malone. I have a funeral to attend." She rose abruptly and opened her office door.

Walking back down the corridor to the exit, I felt as if I had just been given six of the best for snapping a crayon.

Eleven

We turned the corner and immediately the leaning tower was in front of us. I was always amazed by the sight of the church tower bending protectively over the road. It was one of Lincolnshire's quirks and I loved it.

"It looks like there are a lot here, Sir." Shepherd was turning around in his seat, trying to find somewhere for us to park. For as far as the eye could see, cars were parked along the side of the road; the lay-by opposite was full, as were the two pub car-parks. I turned the car around, went back over the bridge and parked down the lane that ran alongside the river.

"This will have to do. It's only a two minute walk to the church."

The church was full and so we squeezed ourselves in the back underneath the bell tower. Looking around, I could see some familiar faces; all of the teachers from the school were there, along with Sarah Harding.

As the coffin was carried into the church I bowed my head, even though I was supposed to be keeping my eyes open for a killer. I couldn't bear to see the despair and loss on the face of Jason Lloyd; I had even less desire to see the faces of the four children. Suddenly, I felt like a voyeur.

"Let's go!"

Grabbing Shepherd's arm, we silently made our way out into the fresh air.

"Are you ok, Sir?"

I sat on a gravestone and ran my hand across my

forehead.

"What are we doing here, lad? This is no place for us. We need to be out there doing something."

Shepherd said nothing as he watched me struggling to contain the emotions that were bubbling inside me.

"Let's get back to the station."

As we headed back down the church path, the soft notes of 'The Lord Is My Shepherd' fluttered out of the church in a wave of sorrow.

Twelve

He rode down the street looking for her house. When he located it, he slowed slightly to get a better look. The house was detached, but it was overlooked by the houses on the opposite side of the road. As he continued, he saw with disappointment that he would not be able to gain access to the rear of the property without being seen. He would need another plan. He would allow her to live a little longer.

By the time I left the station, my mood had not improved. The meeting at the school and my trip to Suzanne Lloyd's funeral had left me feeling inadequate and useless. I didn't like it!

As I turned into the supermarket car-park, a little too sharply, I came face to face with Elsie Johnson. The look of astonishment on her face as I slammed on my brakes brought me to my senses. I wound my window down and leaned out.

"Sorry, Mrs Johnson, my mind was elsewhere. Are you and Mr Johnson keeping ok?" I smiled my widest smile.

"You need to slow down, young man, rushing around like that. You gave me a right turn!"

"Sorry!" I smiled again.

"Just you be careful, Mr Malone, or you'll have an accident." She tottered off on her way to the bus-stop and this time my smile was genuine as I said goodbye. A ticking off from a member of the older generation was just what I had needed.

As I walked to collect my trolley, I pulled out my

trusty notebook to check my shopping list; meals for one and cat food. Although I was a pretty good cook, I usually found that I didn't have the energy or inclination to spend time preparing meals just for me. It was easier and quicker to throw something in the microwave. I replaced the notebook safely in my inside pocket and took my trolley.

As I went through the automatic doors, I knew that in here I would need to keep my wits about me. There is nothing as dangerous as a woman with a trolley. I negotiated my way through the traffic jam at salads and headed towards the chilled cabinets. Cartons of soup with exotic names were at eye level. I picked up one carton of winter vegetable soup and one carton of summer vegetable soup and read the ingredients. The only difference between them was that the summer vegetable soup had a tomato! No wonder it was more expensive. I put it back on the shelf and placed the carton of winter vegetable soup in my trolley.

I continued to bakery, narrowly avoiding a toddler armed with a baguette. As I contemplated the array of bread rolls, wondering which one would be the perfect accompaniment for my winter vegetable soup, I heard and felt a 'clunk' as someone drove in to my trolley. Turning my head, I found myself diving once more into the clear blue eyes of the heavenly doctor.

"Mr Malone! Nice to see the stitches are holding up."

"Yes, they're fine, thanks, Dr ..." I took a breath. "I'm sorry. I never caught your name this morning. Silly of me."

"Fiona Davies."

"Mike Malone."

"I know." She laughed and her face lit up. "I take it you live alone?" She studied my trolley with its solitary carton of soup.

"Not exactly, I do have a cat."

"I love cats!" She smiled again, so I threw caution to the wind and took a chance.

"This may be a bad idea, it may be a truly awful idea," I watched her tilt her head in anticipation, waiting for me to continue, "but when I've finished stocking up on ready-meals and cat food, why don't I buy you a drink?"

"It's not an awful idea at all. I'd like that. Shall I meet you in the car-park in fifteen minutes?"

"Perfect."

I watched her as she continued down the aisle. As she reached the bottom, she turned around and smiled. Shopping had just jumped to the top of my most pleasurable activities list.

Thirteen

He was surprised to find that nothing at the farm had changed; he had expected a little bit more security. The one thing he did remember was the pig's reaction to fire. This time he would not light the candles, he didn't want her raising the alarm.

He placed the cake in front of her and watched her plunge into it. He waited until every last bit of it had been devoured. He waited until she lay down, until she was struggling to maintain her hold on life. Only then did he put the paper hat on her head. As he left the farm he sang 'Happy Birthday' to himself and smiled.

As I drove to the station, I heard my heart singing along with the birds. Everywhere I looked I could see sunshine and I was aware that my face was sporting a huge grin.

At the station, I bounced up the steps; I had a real spring in my step. The world was a wonderful place to be. Nothing could upset me today. Nothing.

"Morning, Sir." Grayson's face was grim. Shepherd was beside him, pacing on the spot in evident distress.

"Beautiful day, isn't it?" I beamed at them. They exchanged a puzzled glance.

"We've had a call, Sir." Shepherd was studying me carefully. "Are you ok, Sir? You seem … different."

"I'm fine, lad. In fact, I am better than fine – I am wonderful."

Grayson and Shepherd exchanged another glance.

"Mr Chambers called fifteen minutes ago, Sir."
Grayson spoke quietly, evidently not wanting to
ruin my good mood. "He found Florrie dead in her
sty this morning. She had been given another
birthday cake."

The balloon burst! My good mood shattered into a
zillion pieces and I heard them dropping to the
ground all around me, like a zillion tiny tinkling
bells.

"He's going back to finish what he started." I
looked at Shepherd who was straining at the leash,
waiting for me to give the order. "We'd better go,
lad. He may have been careless this time, but I
somehow doubt it."

We left the station, leaving the remnants of my
good mood blowing across the station floor like
confetti in a breeze.

Harold Chambers met us we pulled up. His face
showed not only sorrow at the needless death of
Florrie, but also blind rage.

"Why didn't you protect her?" He thundered. He
erupted like a volcano and the heat of his anger
overwhelmed us. "You could have stopped him
from killing her!"

I put my hand on his arm to reassure and comfort,
but he shook me off as if I were an annoying fly.
"After Jim's Rosie was killed, you should have
been looking out for us."

"I'm sorry, Mr Chambers, but we never expected
him to come back and try again. But I will be
stepping up surveillance now."

"Bit bloody late for that, isn't it? My Florrie's

dead and it's your fault."

We watched him storm away and make for the sanctuary of the farmhouse. I could feel the ground shaking as he thumped his way across the yard, anger following in his wake.

"He's right." I turned to Shepherd. "My first thought after Rosie's death should have been to increase the patrols." My conscience roused itself and started pricking me sharply. I enjoyed the pain; it served to remind me that I had failed in my duty to serve and protect.

"So, he'll probably be after Bertha and Sadie now?" Shepherd had his hands in his pockets, he looked crestfallen. Harold Chamber's outburst had also affected him.

"It looks that way. I just wish I knew why he's doing this."

We made our way to the pig-sty where Dan Marshall was waiting for us.

"Morning, Mike. I've not been into her yet, I wanted to wait until you had a chance to check the sty." He held out his hand which I shook warmly. It was nice to see a friendly face.

Shepherd hopped over the wall of the sty and started his fingertip search. Dan and I watched him.

"Another birthday cake, Mike. Do you have any idea who is poisoning the pigs?"

"None at all and there are no clues of any note either."

"Harold is very, very angry."

"I know and I totally understand. I should have put patrols on but I just didn't think that the killer would retrace his steps."

66

"Sir!"

Alan Shepherd was on his knees beside a crushed paper plate; his face was animated.

"What have you got, lad?"

"There's a phone number on the back of the plate."

"Well, ring the shop when you get back and see if they can remember who bought the plates."

"You don't understand, Sir." He pushed himself to his feet and made his way through the mud to join us. "It's not a shop number, Sir. The number has been scribbled down on the plate."

As he turned the plate over, there it was in blue ink. A phone number. A local phone number. At last, the killer had made a mistake.

"Well done, lad. Have another scout around to see if there is anything else, and then let's get out of here."

"Yes, Sir."

I looked up into the morning sky and saw the grey clouds beginning to break. Was this the breakthrough that I was waiting for?

As soon as Shepherd had cleaned himself up, he came to join me in my office. As I was still considered by many in the town to be a newcomer - not a local - I valued Shepherd's help when it came to dealing with the general public. I found that he often had their confidence, whilst I had the backs of their heads. I dialled the number that had been written on the plate and waited. On the third ring it was answered; the voice was female.

"Hello?"

67

"This is Detective Inspector Malone. Who am ..."

"Oh my God! Has there been an accident?" She was gasping for breath. Once again, I had jumped in with both feet and caused distress. I passed the phone over to Shepherd and listened to the conversation.

"Hello! This is Alan Shepherd."

Immediately, I could hear the voice on the other end of the phone calming down. Unfortunately, I couldn't hear what she was saying. I pushed my blotter and pen over to Shepherd.

"Sorry," he said into the receiver, "who is this?"

The suspense was killing me. It was like watching a B rated horror movie from the fifties and waiting for the alien to appear in the window.

"Vera! I'm sorry. I didn't recognise your voice. Yes, I'm fine thanks. How are you?"

He scribbled a name on the blotter and pushed it back to me. Vera Rington. Who the devil was Vera Rington? I put three question marks beside the name and pushed it back to him.

"No," he was saying, "I haven't seen Sam since he left after Christmas. What about Lynn? Have you seen her recently?"

I put my head in my hands and screamed silently. Shepherd was catching up on local gossip! I didn't want to know where Sam was and actually, I didn't really care what Lynn had been up to. I wanted to know who Vera Rington was!

"Really," he continued, "they were dating when we were at school. I always thought that they would end up walking down the aisle together. How did she take it? ... She didn't? Good for her!"

I could stand it no longer. Reaching for the blotter, I scrawled in big, bold letters 'MURDER!' and pushed it back to Shepherd, making sure that it hit him on the arm. He glanced down at it and turned pink with embarrassment.

"Anyway, Vera," he interrupted her story, "the reason that I am ringing is that D.I. Malone thinks that you might be able to help us. Yes, the Suzanne Lloyd murder... Yes, I know about Florrie, that's the reason I rang. Your phone number was found in Florrie's sty written on a paper plate. Have you, by any chance, had any strange phone calls in the past few days?"

He turned to me and mouthed the word 'sorry'. As I did not change the expression on my face, he looked quickly away.

"When was that?... Did he leave a name?... Did he say anything else?... Ok, thank you. It was nice to chat and catch up a bit. Take care. Bye."

He put the receiver down and turned back towards me.

"Sorry, Sir. I just got carried away."

"Evidently! This is a murder enquiry, lad, or had you forgotten?"

"No, Sir. I'm sorry. Anyway, Vera Rington is the receptionist at the doctor's surgery. She ..."

"That bad-tempered woman we saw yesterday?"

"No. That was Edna, Vera only works two days a week. She said that a couple of days ago she had a phone call from a man who wanted to know if he was speaking to Vera, and he also wanted to know if she was still working at the surgery. He didn't give a name and when Vera tried to ask a question, he hung up. She didn't recognise the voice, but said that he was nicely spoken."

"It might be innocent, but why the question about if she was still working at the surgery?"

"You don't think, do you, Sir? That she …"

I sat back in my chair and let thoughts loose to run around my brain. I waited as they weighed up all the possibilities, discarded ideas and jumped to conclusions. Finally, the jury reached a verdict upon which they all agreed, and they posted the note into my mind.

"I let Florrie die! If there is even the remotest chance that this man is after Vera, and I have no idea why he should be after her, then…" I stopped and took a breath. "I do not want any more blood on my hands. I'm going to post a patrol outside Vera's. I can't afford not to, she might be next on his list."

"I agree, Sir. The phone call was pretty odd. What about the pigs?"

"I'll sort out patrols to go around the farms as well. Bring me the duty rota, will you?"

By the end of the morning everything had been arranged. A car would be outside Vera's day and night; three extra cars would be patrolling the farms. I had everything covered.

Fourteen

I loved this time of the evening; I would never tire of Lincolnshire's dramatic sunsets. In London it was so different. The sun was there, the sun was gone. It was as if God had a light switch. Living here for the past few months had made me appreciate my surroundings; the big skies that gradually changed as the sun disappeared over the horizon. At this rate, I would soon be taking up bird-watching. God forbid!

Ophelia was stretched across her chair, waiting for me to settle down for the evening so that she could leap onto my chest. I turned to my bookcase and ran my fingers over the well-loved spines; romance, comedy, tragedy. I stopped at 'Hamlet' and taking the text from the shelf, I settled down to read. As I knew she would, Ophelia climbed onto my chest, kneaded me gently for a moment and then lay down to listen to Hamlet's soliloquies.

I had hardly started reading when the sound of the telephone transported me back from Elsinore to reality. Ophelia lifted her head and glared at the phone before jumping off me to reclaim her chair.

"Malone." I waited with baited breath. Was this another pig murder or something more dreadful?

"Mike, it's Martin Goddard."

My heart sank. Badminton!

"Hello, Martin. What can I do for you?"

"Two things. First – how's the head?"

"Fine, thanks. I think I did more damage to the court" My laugh was forced and I heard a similarly forced chuckle in reply.

"Good. Number two – has Simon been in touch with you?"

"No. Should he have done?" My heart got into the lift and pressed the button to Hell.

"He did say that he was going to. Never mind, I'll pass the message on. The court is rebooked for tomorrow night. Eight o'clock. Are you free?"

The lift came to a juddering halt and the door opened. I had arrived in Hell. "I'm free and already looking forward to a re-match."

"Brilliant! Let's hope it's not so eventful this time. See you tomorrow."

I put the phone down. Picking up my book from the sofa arm, I put it back on the shelf. I was no longer in the mood for 'Hamlet'; I picked up Dante's 'Inferno'.

Fifteen

He drove by Martin Webb's farm and spotted the police car. He laughed and carried on his way down the lane; his mission was too important to be knocked off course by a patrol car. A quick check in his rear view mirror told him that he wasn't being followed. At the bottom of the lane he took a left turn and headed for Nigel Henson's.

The morning sun was playing hide and seek as I drove to the station. I didn't mind. I had a lunch date to look forward to. Fiona had phoned me before she left for the surgery to check up on my stitches, allegedly. I knew different. I knew that the old Malone charm had worked its magic! We had agreed to meet for lunch at Giorgio's tomorrow after her rounds, unless I was detained by a case. But why wait till tomorrow? Why not invite her to meet me after the badminton game tonight?

The crash in my head brought me to my senses as reality fell on its back laughing hysterically and kicking its legs in the air. Bad idea! I wanted to impress her with my intellect, not put her off with my lack of physical fitness. I wanted her to see me as calm, pleasant and happy not red-faced, gasping and wheezing. Better stick to the original plan and meet her tomorrow.

Shepherd was waiting for me with an armful of plastic bags and two pairs of wellingtons. Not another one!

"Oh no, lad! Not Sadie?"

He shook his head. "No, Sir. It's Nigel Henson's.

This time he has poisoned both of their pigs."

Nigel Henson's farm was on the edge of town. He was not of farming stock. He and his wife, Rita, had moved to the country fifteen years ago. He had been a stockbroker in the City and having made himself a little nest-egg, he had decided that he wanted to escape from the rat-race. Rita had given up her career as a solicitor and they had settled here and built up the farm from nothing. They were a popular couple and heavily involved with the Parish Council and various committees. I couldn't imagine who would want to target them.

Nigel was in the yard talking to Dan Marshall as we arrived. They came over to meet us.

"Morning, Mike. I won't say 'good' if you don't mind." Dan's face was grim.

Shaking his hand, I turned to Nigel Henson. His dark wavy hair was falling into his eyes and he brushed it away.

"Mr Malone. Glad you could come so quickly."

"It's a mess, Mike." Dan looked across the yard to the sty. "It's poison again. It looks as if Viola had most of the cake, but Echo is still quite sick."

"Viola is …" I already knew the answer.

"Viola's dead, Mr Malone." Nigel Henson put his hands in his pockets and turned towards the sty. "Come and look for yourself."

When we got to the sty the first thing that I noticed, apart two pigs, was that there only appeared to have been one cake. I had been expecting to see two – one for each pig. I turned to Shepherd.

"Have a good look around, lad. See if you can confirm that there was just the one cake."

Shepherd had already put his wellingtons on and was clambering over the wall into the sty.

"I only saw one plate, Mr Malone. What are you thinking?" Nigel Henson was trying to read answers on my face.

"Nothing at the moment," I lied. "Just trying to get all the facts."

I wasn't going to tell him what I was really thinking; that his farm had not been the target, but the sight of the patrol car had diverted our poisoner here. After all, he had previously planned his 'birthday parties' so carefully, he would have made sure that there was enough poison for two pigs; he would certainly have brought two cakes. No, I would not tell him that his pigs were the second choice dish on the menu.

I turned to Dan. "Will Echo be alright?"

"She should be. I've given her a shot. I don't think that she could have had too much cake. Viola, being the older sow, would have pushed her away. Echo would have got the left-overs."

I nodded and turned back to Shepherd who at that moment was scrapping straw away from the rear wall. He had found something!

"Sir, look at this!"

I entered the sty, taking care not to step on the suffering Echo, and bent down next to him.

"Fresh blood, Sir. It's been covered with straw to hide it."

"Good work, lad." I stood up and looked towards Dan. "Tell me, Dan, were the pigs injured in any way? Shepherd has found blood."

"No injuries at all, Mike."

"Echo doesn't like strangers," Nigel interrupted. "If someone entered the sty, she would have gone for him. She has a temper on her, bless her. She has even nipped me in the past."

I bent down again to Shepherd. "Take a sample for tests, lad. You know what this means, don't you?"

"What, Sir?"

"We are now looking for someone with dark curly hair, glasses and a bandage. Let's get back to the station and circulate the description."

Sixteen

Sitting on the edge of the bath, he cut his trousers away from the bite and carefully cleaned the wound. The pig's teeth had sunk deep into his flesh. Damn it! Unfortunately there had not been enough cake to kill it too. But, he would get his revenge. After bandaging his thigh, he stood painfully and looked at himself in the mirror. With a smile, he picked up his phone and dialled.

I decided to treat Shepherd to lunch as a reward for finding the blood and we stopped at The King's Head on our way back. He chose a table in the corner while I went to the bar to order a couple of pints and two steak sandwiches.

"Morning, Mike. What's with the plaster?" Frank Bassett couldn't take his eyes off my forehead.

"Badminton injury."

"Stick to darts, Mike," he laughed. "A lot safer and you can have a couple of pints while you're playing."

"But don't darts have sharp points, Frank?" I gave him a look of mock seriousness. "Dominoes will have to be my game in the future – after tonight's rematch of course."

"Ah, you want to get matching plasters, do you?" Frank winked as he put the first pint in front of me,

"Actually, Frank, what I'm planning to do is to try and keep out of trouble."

"You do that Mike. I'll bring your lunches over."

Putting Shepherd's pint in front of him, I settled myself down.

"Now, lad, we need a plan."

"I agree, Sir." He leaned forward. "Shall I ring around the surgeries and A&E when we get back to see if anyone has needed a bite attending to?"

"Not that sort of plan." He looked at me, puzzled. "A plan to get me out of tonight's badminton game."

"And I thought you were wanting to get fit, Sir."

"Simon wanted to get fit. I am quite happy as I am." I took a sip of beer and gave Shepherd a look that challenged him to contradict me.

"And we are happy with you as you are too, Sir," he grinned. "Grumpy, bad-tempered and …"

"A bloody good boss!"

"That was just what I was going to say."

Further conversation was halted by the arrival of our lunches and a contented silence fell upon our table.

"Oh, sorry to hear that, Mike," Simon seemed genuinely concerned about the fact that my stitches were not healing and that I had been advised to take thinks easy. I had my fingers crossed beneath the table and Shepherd was enjoying watching me lying through my teeth. "Actually, I was going to ring you anyway to tell you that the game had been cancelled. Richard has come down with a tummy bug and Martin's business meeting in Stockport looks as if it will run over and he won't get back in time."

"What a shame!" I tried to keep my voice sincere; I could hear Shepherd tutting and turned my back on him. "I was really looking forward to it."

"We'll make it another time, Mike. Take care of that head – we need our policemen to be fully functioning to sort out these murders."

"I'll see you around, Simon. Maybe we can meet for a drink next week?"

I put the phone down, slowly. Simon's last remark had felt like a criticism, a criticism that I was not fully functioning as this murderer was continuing his trade unchecked. My joviality had gone and Shepherd, sensing instantly my change of mood, headed for the office door.

"I'll see if there is any news from A&E, Sir."

"You do that, lad."

Alone once again, I wandered over to the crime-board. What was I missing? After studying it for a few moments, I returned to the desk to start my paperwork.

As the cancellation of the badminton match gave me a free evening, I had two choices. I could either sit with Ophelia in my cottage or I could phone Fiona to see if she wanted to meet tonight instead of tomorrow lunchtime. Drawing a line down the centre of my blotter, I decided to list advantages and disadvantages for meeting her tonight. 'Desperate' was the first word that my subconscious wrote down. It was quickly followed by 'eager' and 'controlling'. I ripped the sheet off, tore it into several tiny pieces and threw them in the air. Closing my eyes, I pictured Fiona's liquid blue eyes and her tender smile. I could feel myself relax just thinking about her. With a sigh I opened my eyes and smiled. The ripped up pieces of paper had formed a single word on the blotter in front of me; 'romantic'. I reached for the phone.

Seventeen

As the daylight began to fade, he looked up from his hiding place. Good! The bicycle was well hidden. He checked his watch. Ten minutes to go. His limbs had frozen in position and the wound from the bite was throbbing. He wanted to stretch, to enjoy the luxurious pain as the blood began to flow again, but he couldn't. The patrol car would be passing by very soon and he didn't want to risk being seen. The gentle hum of a car engine in the distance caused his heart rate to quicken. He held his breath and pushed himself deeper into the hedgerow. Twigs scratched the soft skin on the back of his neck; a fly, angry at being disturbed, batted his cheek. His lungs were straining, as the air bubbled within him, trying to escape. The car came closer. A swoosh of air and it had passed, leaving the smell of pollution in its wake. He opened his mouth and expelled the air that he had trapped within him. Uncurling his limbs, he slowly got to his feet and stretched. The exquisite pull on his muscles excited him and he smiled.

Access had been so easy. As he looked down on her sleeping form, he listened to the gentle rhythm of her breathing and wondered if she was dreaming. It would be a shame to awaken her, but he wanted her to see him. He wanted her to recognise him and to know that she was going to die. He wanted to see the life in her eyes snuffed out like a candle, to be the last thing she would ever see.

He touched her gently and her eyes opened and

*focused on him. He saw uncertainty, confusion. She
didn't recognise him! Anger boiled within him. He
had wanted her to know him, to know why she was
to die. He had wanted her to acknowledge her own
role in her death. He moved closer. He moved into
the last remaining light of the day so that she could
really see him. Her expression changed instantly.
Fear flooded her face and her eyes swam with tears.
Then, surprisingly he saw anger pushing the fear
aside. She started to pull herself up. She started to
confront him. She started to open her mouth. Her
skull cracked beneath the axe and split like an egg.
He watched the blood rush out like lava from a
volcano. The light in her eyes went out and he
laughed. He was still laughing as he got back on his
bike and rode slowly away.*

I sat back and studied Fiona over the top of my
menu. In the warm lighting of Giorgio's, she looked
radiant. Her hair sparkled as if made of starlight. As
she read the menu, she rested her cheek on her hand
and I felt like Romeo watching Juliet on the balcony
and wanting to be her hand.

"This was such a good idea, Mike. I'm glad you
phoned." Her smile was genuine and soft. "What do
you recommend?"

"I'm a mushroom man myself."

"Does that mean that you live in a toadstool?"
Laughter radiated from her eyes.

"No, but I have my very own fairy ring in the
garden."

"You'll have to show me."

I looked into her eyes and stopped breathing.

"That can be arranged."

"Well, I'm going to skip the starter, if you don't mind. I'll sit and watch you eat your mushrooms."

"We could always share some garlic bread?"

"Sounds good."

The waitress came over and hovered like an annoying bluebottle.

"Are you ready to order?" Her voice even had the buzz of an annoying bluebottle.

Fiona smiled at me and inclined her head. Her blonde hair caressed her bare shoulder and I watched, entranced.

"No starter for me. I'll just have the *penne con salmone*, please." Fiona's voice awakened me from my close study of her soft skin and I blushed.

"I'll have the baked mushrooms for starter, followed by *penne al pollo zafferano*. Can we have some garlic bread with the starter please?"

"Do you want any wine?" That voice buzzed again.

"Shall we?" I looked across at Fiona who smiled encouragingly. Picking up the wine list, I scanned it quickly and found just what I was looking for. "The Sicilian Chardonnay, please."

The waitress scratched the order onto her pad and left.

"Now where were we?" I leaned towards Fiona. "Oh yes, we were discussing my fairy ring."

As we left the restaurant, Fiona put her hand under my arm.

"That was a lovely evening, Mike. Thank you."

"My pleasure, and of course the company was

exceptional."

I felt her eyes on me but I didn't have the courage to look at her.

"It's a beautiful evening, Mike. Shall we go for a walk by the river?"

"Not in this town, unless you want to step over the local drunks. But I know just the place, if you don't mind a little drive?"

"Perfect."

As I put my key into the car door, a movement caught my eye, and looking round I saw Martin Goddard closing the boot of his BMW.

"Martin!" As I raised my hand to wave, I saw him look around like a startled rabbit. Upon seeing me, he relaxed and walked over to join us. We shook hands.

"Sorry, about tonight, Mike. Business meetings! What can you say?"

"No problem." I turned towards Fiona. "You know Fiona Davies, don't you?"

I was surprised to see a shutter close over his face. His expression became frozen like ice.

"Yes. I know her!" The words crept from his lips. He slapped me on the back and returned to his car without another word.

I turned to Fiona, totally bewildered by what had just happened, and saw that the light had disappeared from her eyes. Even in the glow of the street-light, I could see that sadness had pushed its way on to her cheek. I opened the door and she slid into the passenger seat. As I got in beside her, she put her hand on mine.

"Would you be dreadfully disappointed if I said

that I had changed my mind about the walk?"

I squeezed her hand gently.

"Of course not," I lied. "You'd probably have been disappointed anyway. The Welland is not the most picturesque of rivers. Now, a midnight walk beside the River Cam is a much more romantic setting."

"I'd like that, Mike. Maybe we can do that one day." Her hand was trembling in mine.

"Look, Fiona, tell me to mind my own business, but what is it?"

The sadness was back in her eyes and a single tear glistened on her cheek.

"Old memories, Mike. Old memories."

That explained it. Martin Goddard was an ex-lover, and judging by her reaction, someone that she had evidently cared a great deal for. As I watched the BMW make its way out of the car-park, I noticed that Fiona was also watching it. Only when its rear lights had disappeared into the distance did I hear her breathe again.

Eighteen

The phone woke me at five thirty. I say it woke me, but in reality it interrupted a dream of Fiona and I walking hand in hand along a Venetian canal, bathed in silver moonlight. I stretched out an arm to locate my phone and found it on the second attempt.

"Malone."

"Sir, it's Shepherd. You'd better come over to Nigel Henson's"

The darkness in Shepherd's voice told me that I didn't need to ask any more questions. Throwing back the duvet, I swung my legs over the side of the bed and prepared my mind for the horror that I felt sure was waiting for me.

As I turned off the engine, Shepherd opened the car door.

"It's bad, Sir, really bad!"

After the horrors that Shepherd had witnessed a few months ago, I would have thought that nothing further could shock him. One glance at his cheeks, which were as pale as parchment, showed me that I was wrong.

Following in his footsteps, I approached the pig-sty. I saw the anger on Dan Marshall's face. I saw the grief in Nigel Henson's eyes. I saw shock on the face of Constable Brooks, who had been first on the scene. This was certainly no birthday party.

I thought myself hardened to sights of horror, but the scene in the pig-sty made even my blood still in my veins. Echo's body was lying in a pool of slowly congealing blood. Echo's head was on the feeding trough. An axe had been driven into her skull, splitting her face down the centre so that her sightless eyes looked in different directions. Over what remained of her snout, there hung a green party hat.

"Jesus!" I could find no words to express my thoughts. "When did..."

"I popped over to check on her before I locked up for the night – about eight. Why, Mr Malone? She was a good little pig. Why do this to her?"

I had no comforting words to give him so I said nothing.

"You've got to get this maniac, Mike. He's out of control." Dan hissed, anger bouncing off every word.

"Unfortunately, Dan, I think it's the opposite. He is very much in control. He knows exactly what he is doing and why." My eyes were still fixed to the spectacle of Echo's head. "I just wish I had some clue to tell me who he is, but he leaves nothing behind."

"But this is evil."

"This is revenge, Dan. Echo bit him, remember?" I turned to Shepherd. "Have a nose around, lad, see what you can find."

As Shepherd opened the gate, I turned back to Nigel Henson, put my arm under his and led him back to the farmhouse. Dan Marshall stayed with Echo.

The kitchen was warm, inviting and filled with the aroma of frying bacon.

"Bacon sandwich, Mr Malone?" Rita brushed her

dark hair from her eyes and smiled at me; her mouth smiled, her eyes reflected her sorrow.

"Not at the moment, Mrs Henson, thank you."

"I'll have one, love. I need something to stop me thinking about poor Echo."

The drawer in my mind where I store odd facts opened. I scribbled a hasty note and filed it. Question: what does a farmer do when dealing with the horrific mutilation of a favourite sow? Answer: eat a bacon sandwich. With the drawer shut again, I turned back to Nigel Henson who at that moment had a mouth full of pig flesh while spots of blood red tomato ketchup dotted his lips and chin. It was enough to turn me vegetarian.

Back at the station, I added more photographs and notes to the increasingly cluttered crime-board. There had to be something that I was not seeing. My questioning of Nigel and Rita Henson had provided nothing. They had seen nothing. They had heard nothing. However, Shepherd had once again proved exactly why he was so good on his hands and knees. Stuck to the blood around Echo's body, he had found part of a receipt for The Lemon Tree restaurant. This restaurant was well known to me but I had never frequented it. Only when the PM decided to increase my pay would I be able to afford to go there for a meal. At the present moment in time, I would barely be able to afford a drink to go with the complimentary nibbles. As Nigel and Rita had never eaten there either, then it must have fallen from the pocket of the 'butcher' when he had knelt to remove Echo's head. Therefore, the killer

88

was someone who had enough money to be able to eat at The Lemon Tree. The search was narrowing.

I turned as Shepherd came in with a mug of tea and some hot buttered toast.

"How many of your friends eat at The Lemon Tree, lad?"

"None! In fact, I can't think of anyone that I know ever eating there."

"Simon told me once that the Prince of Wales was a regular visitor."

"He can afford to be. Cat and I looked at the menu once – over forty pounds for a steak!"

"Sit down, lad. I want to ask you something."

Shepherd looked at me with surprise. He could see that I had my serious face on and I watched as a wave of concern floated over his face.

"You've lived here a long time."

"You know I have, Sir."

"What can you tell me about Martin Goddard and Fiona Davies."

"In what way?"

"They were in a relationship."

"Were they? Are you sure? He doesn't seem her type."

I hid a smile behind my hand. "And what is her type?"

"I've only met her a couple of times, Sir, one of them when I went with you. But, I should think her type is someone who is intelligent and funny. Someone who has some life. Goddard is a limp lettuce. He's totally wet!"

My smile got larger and peeped around the sides of my hand. Immediately, I saw a light bulb come on in Shepherd's eyes."

"Sir! You and Dr Davies?"

"We're just friends, lad."

"I believe you, Sir." He winked. "Wow! Wait till I tell Cat."

"Don't!" Shepherd looked at me in astonishment. "Not yet, we've only been out once and … you know."

He nodded with the wisdom of his years sitting on his shoulders.

"I won't say a word, Sir. Doctor's orders." He grinned.

"Very funny!" I smiled. "But returning to my original question, when we bumped into Goddard last night, he was very cold towards Fi … Dr Davies. She was quite upset."

"I never heard any gossip about them at all. But remember that Dr Davies has only recently come back."

"Come back?"

"She came as a locum a couple of years ago when old Dr Foreman went down with swine flu. I suppose they could have been seeing each other. As she wasn't living here then we would never have known. Goddard is not one for being out and about. He keeps himself very private."

"That's possible. If that's the case, he wouldn't be too happy about her coming back to live on his doorstep."

Shepherd drummed his fingers on my desk, thinking.

"I'll ask around, Sir. Quietly."

"You do that."

After a lunch consisting of a cheese and pickle sandwich which I had picked up from Jennings' newsagents when I had popped in to buy a paper, I rang The Lemon Tree. As I was waiting to be connected to the manager, I suddenly realised how stupid my phone call was going to sound. What was I going to ask him? Is there anyone among your clientele who you would consider to be a killer? Have you ever served anyone with blood on their shoes?

"Lawrence West, speaking. How can I help you, Mr Malone?" A well polished voice interrupted my thoughts.

"Er, do you have a quiet table for two for this evening? I know it is short notice."

"Would eight forty-five be acceptable, Mr Malone?"

"That would be perfect. Thank you."

I disconnected the call and dialled Fiona's number. What had Shepherd said? Over forty pounds for a steak? Oh well, I would only disappoint my bank manager if I didn't take full advantage of my overdraft.

The evening sunlight glistened on the water and as I walked along the riverbank with Fiona by my side, I felt as if life couldn't get any better. She smiled at me.

"What a super idea, Mike."

"It's a lovely walk at this time of year. And, didn't I promise you a romantic river walk last night?"

She squeezed my hand and we continued in

91

silence. A barking in the distance disturbed my thoughts, and my balance. Fiona had grabbed hold of my arm so tightly that I had stumbled and had almost found myself on my knees.

"Mike, I'm frightened." She was pale with fear.

"What?" I looked around, bemused. On a perfect evening like this with only the sound of a warbler singing in the reeds, what was there to be frightened of?

"A dog, Mike. I'm frightened of dogs."

I was going to laugh, but the sight of her terrified eyes stopped the laughter in my throat.

"Stand this side of me, I'll look after you."

I pulled her gently to my right side, and with my arm firmly around her, we continued. I could hear panic in her breathing as we got nearer to the bend.

Under the branches of the overhanging tree we met the dog. An aging spaniel was sitting beside its owner, looking just as frightened as Fiona.

"Evening," a deep voice laughed. "The way Cilla was barking, I thought you must be a couple of alsations."

"Not us, we're quite harmless." I laughed as we passed him and I felt Fiona relax beside me.

"I'm sorry, Mike. It's just my thing. Some people are afraid of spiders, I'm afraid of dogs."

I kissed her cheek and we continued towards the village.

"Look, Mike. A couple of terns."

"Brilliant!" I said without looking. I had just seen in the distance a figure coming towards us. A figure with not one, but three dogs! So much for my good idea for a nice romantic walk!

The evening at The Lemon Tree had been wonderful; wonderfully expensive, but just perfect. Fiona had been relaxed, sparkling, amusing; there was no sign of the tension that Martin Goddard had caused yesterday. I could also say that for the first time in a very long time I had felt happy. Fiona made me laugh, mainly at myself. As I paid the bill, I saw the manager, Lawrence West, checking the optics at the bar. Whispering to Fiona that I just needed to see him, I made my way over to join him. Our taxi hadn't arrived, so I had a couple of minutes.

"Mr West."

He turned towards me and observed me from over the top of his gold-rimmed spectacles.

"Mr Malone. I trust that you enjoyed your evening?" His voice was oily and patronising. I felt the hairs on my spine instantly rise; I didn't appreciate being spoken down to.

"Excellent! I was just wondering, in my official capacity, if you keep a record of diners."

"A record of our clientele? Why?" Dislike and distrust jockeyed for prime position as he observed me coldly.

"I am investigating the murder of Suzanne Lloyd, as you are no doubt aware. A receipt for this restaurant was found at the murder scene," I lied. He didn't need to know which murder scene. "It would be very helpful to our enquiries to see who was dining here on the sixth of June."

"If my memory serves me correctly, Mr Malone, the murder occurred after the sixth of June."

I swallowed back my dislike and smiled sweetly. "I am aware of that Mr West. My point is that this receipt was dropped at the scene by the killer and it would be helpful to see who it might have belonged to."

"Our restaurant list is confidential, Mr Malone."

"This is a murder enquiry, Mr West."

"I am not going to allow you to harass my clientele unnecessarily. That receipt is the flimsiest piece of evidence; it could have blown in from anywhere."

"So you are not going to help me?"

"No, I'm afraid I am not. Good night, Mr Malone." He turned away and continued to check the optics. I had been dismissed.

As I returned to Fiona's side, she saw instantly that the conversation had not gone well. She took my hand and caressed my fingers.

"Unhelpful?" she whispered as we left the restaurant and headed for the waiting taxi.

"Extremely. But I'll be back with a warrant."

"Good. Let's forget all about that horrible little man and enjoy the rest of the evening."

Nineteen

He let the patrol car get to the end of the lane before he slipped into the farmyard. In the pigsty, the pig was asleep. He looked at it with loathing. It had made a fool of him; now he would have the last laugh. As silently as a cat, he crept up beside her and plunged the knife into her throat. The gentle snuffling of sleep was replaced by gurgling gasps as the pig tried to scramble to its feet. As the blood soaked the straw she had been sleeping on, the fight went out of her and she lay down beaten. He watched the light leave her eyes. She was dead. Her life was over, but, his fun had just begun.

I switched the alarm off, turned over and smiled at her. Fiona's hair had fallen over her eyes and I tenderly lifted it to one side. She smiled.

"Morning."

"Good morning." I kissed her forehead. "Would you like a cup of tea?"

"That would be lovely." She put her hand on my arm to stop me as I tried to get out of bed. "Mike?" I saw anxiety in her eyes. I knew it was too good to be true. She was going to dump me!

"Mm!"

"Who's David?"

I froze and looked at her. Concern had been joined by compassion and understanding on her face. I could find no words. I could only feel tears threatening to fill my eyes. I swallowed, trying to keep them in their place, trying to ease the tightness in my throat.

"Mike, who's David?" Her voice was tender, gentle, caring. "You were calling his name in your sleep. You were in tears and I couldn't wake you. You frightened me."

I swallowed again and then looked at her.

"David is … was my son." I had spoken the words that I had tried to keep locked behind that door in my memory, the door that needed to be made secure. I dropped my head, I couldn't look at her. As I straightened the creases in the duvet, I felt her hand stroke my cheek and she gently raised my head until I was looking at her.

"Oh, Mike!" Concern, compassion and understanding wrapped themselves around me like a blanket. "I won't ask any questions. But if you want to talk, I'll be here."

She drew me to her and I clung to her as if I was drowning, as if she were my life-belt. I hung onto her and I sobbed.

When I entered my cottage forty-five minutes later, I was aware of two things. Firstly, Ophelia was giving me the cold shoulder after being abandoned all night; secondly, the red light on my answer-phone was flashing. The second problem was easy to solve. I pressed the button and heard Grayson's hesitant voice. Poor Grayson was not at all comfortable with technology. However the message that he was timidly delivering was clear enough. Bertha, Fred Greengrass' pig had been found horribly mutilated; Grayson announced that he would contact Shepherd as he hadn't been able to reach me. The message was timed at five past four, three and a half hours ago.

Was this chap determined to slaughter every pig in town? It had seemed like such an innocent prank in the beginning – birthday cakes for pigs. Now it had turned into something horrific and murderous. I shuddered to think what his next move might be.

When I went into the kitchen, Ophelia was in her basket facing the wall. I knelt down and tickled her under her chin. No response. I ran my fingers over her ears. No response. She definitely was in a sulk. I had one more trick up my sleeve and if this didn't work, I might as well give up and move out. I ran my hand over her fur and tickled her tummy. Immediately, she rolled over purring loudly. I was forgiven; I picked her up and buried my face in her fur. Dropping a kiss on the top of her head, I set her down next to her food bowl, filled it and left for the station with the sounds of gentle lapping in my ears.

Shepherd was examining the crime-board when I arrived. Several photographs of Bertha were scattered over my desk and I recoiled in horror at the images before me. Bertha was lying on her side in a pool of blood; the gaping wound in her throat showing how she had died. That was bad enough, but carved deep into her flesh were the words 'Happy Birthday'. Worse still, eight pink candles had been pushed into the top of her head. He had turned her into a grotesque parody of a birthday cake.

"Good God, lad! What a mess!"

Alan Shepherd turned around.

"Morning, Sir. Dan says that the carving and the

97

candles were post-mortem. She would have died as
soon as her throat was cut."

"Thank goodness for that. Anything else?"

"Fred didn't see or hear anything. He checked the
yard at about half-past eleven and everything was
ok."

"And?" I could tell from his expression that he
was holding the cherry from the birthday cake in his
hand.

"A clear bloody hand print was left on Bertha's
skin. He must have put his hand out to steady
himself."

"So what can we find out?"

"It was his left hand and he wasn't wearing a
ring."

"So he's not married."

"Not all married men wear a ring, Sir."

"True! What about fingerprints?"

"The lab is checking."

"So our new description is that he has short, wavy
dark hair and wears glasses. He probably has a
bandage or a dressing on his leg and he doesn't
wear a wedding ring."

"Correct."

"Good work. Circulate the new description as
soon as possible."

At lunchtime, I called into The King's Head and
noticed Richard Austin sitting behind a plate of
gammon and chips. I decided to join him.

"Richard, how are you? Recovered from the
tummy bug?"

"Mike!" He looked up and studied me carefully.

"I should be asking after you. It was a nasty bang you had the other night."

"I had worse in my youth." I laughed heartily and sat down.

"So when is the game being arranged for now?" He was busy cutting his gammon and did not see my eyes roll heavenward.

"Never, I hope!"

"What?" He almost dropped his fork in surprise.

"Look at me, Richard. I'm not sporty, I'm certainly not fit. I need to talk Simon out of this crazy idea," I was in deadly earnest, "because if this game goes ahead, then there is a very real chance that I might actually die."

Richard had just taken a mouthful of gammon and the shock of my statement sent it flying across the table. He coughed, spluttered and then burst into laughter.

"First class, Mike! I feel exactly the same. I can't keep up with Martin. I say we stick together, make a united front and say no."

"Glad you're on my side, Richard." I held out my hand and he shook it firmly. The pact was sealed just as my chicken and mushroom pie was placed in front of me.

For a few moments we ate in companionable silence, but then curiosity finally let the cat escape.

"Richard, I need to ask you something."

He put down his cutlery and looked at me; his eyebrows were knitted together in concentration.

"Is this to do with the case?"

"No, it's a personal matter."

He relaxed and picked up his knife and fork again.

"I'm interested in Martin Goddard."

The knife and fork were dropped again and his eyes widened in amazement. He leaned over. "Sorry, Mike," he whispered, "I didn't realise you were ... Anyway, Martin is actually straight."

"What!" This time it was my turn to drop my knife and fork. "No! No, I'm not! What I wanted to ask you is… It's about Fiona Davies. I was out with her the other night and …"

"Dr Davies! Well, you really are a dark horse, Mike. She has caught the eye of many of the men in town. You sly old fox!" He punched me on the arm.

Blushing fiercely, I continued, trying to keep pride out of my voice. "I believe that Martin and Fiona had a thing. We bumped into Martin and the atmosphere between them was very chilly."

"Martin and the luscious doctor! You've got that wrong, Mike."

"Why?"

"I've known Martin for years; he hasn't looked at another woman since Celia walked out on him."

"Celia was his wife?"

"Yes. She had a fling with one of the partners and they ran off to Spain. Martin was left with the daughter. It must have been four or five years ago."

"He could have kept a relationship secret."

"Not old Martin. He wears his heart on his sleeve, always has."

Richard was now into story-telling mode and I knew from the expression on his face that he would continue until the story was told. It was a face I had seen many times before. I picked up my knife and fork and listened as I ate.

"The firm used to be Baker Goddard and Brady. However, Simon Brady had an eye for the ladies – well, one lady in particular, Celia Goddard. He left his wife and she left Martin and the daughter. Poor chap had no idea. He went home one night and most of the furniture had been moved out. She left him a note telling him that the kid was at the childminder's and she was in Spain. It crushed him. He was devoted to her, they had been childhood sweethearts. If it hadn't been for the kid, well I don't know what he would have done. She gave him a reason to keep going."

Richard paused for a breath and a couple more mouthfuls of gammon. As I had had chance to clear my plate, I took advantage of the intermission to ask a question.

"So how old is his daughter now?"

"Poor little thing died two years ago."

"Jesus!" I was shocked. Martin Goddard did not have the air of a man who had lost a child and I should know very well what one looked like;

I saw one every day in the bathroom mirror. "So what about Dr Davies? Are you sure they never had a 'thing'?"

"Never heard any gossip whatsoever. Another pint?"

He got up and went to the bar, leaving me still no closer to finding out the truth about Fiona and Martin.

Twenty

It had been easier to get into the garage than he had thought; carrying a clipboard had been a stroke of genius, after all, who would take notice of the man who read the electricity meters?

Twenty-five past six. Surgery would have finished ten minutes ago. He heard the sound of a car approaching and pressed himself into the corner. The automatic door opened and daylight spilled into the garage, illuminating all but him. Slowly, the car entered. Slowly, the garage door lowered. Slowly, darkness once again gained supremacy.

He edged his way towards the rear of the car, keeping close to the wall. He watched as she opened the car door. He watched as she stepped out. He watched her body freeze as he slipped the ribbon around her neck. He watched her hands clawing at her throat as he tightened the ribbon. He watched her body struggling to break free. He watched her limbs stop fighting and concede defeat. Finally, he released his grip and she sank to the floor, just as he heard wheels on the gravel. Prising the house keys from her hand, he unlocked the connecting door and stepped into an untidy utility room. Looking quickly around, he saw that the door to the garden could be easily forced and within seconds he was outside. He walked back out of the drive and past the parked patrol car; the constable never even looked up from his newspaper.

As he turned left at the bottom of the road, he stopped. As he had had to leave quickly he hadn't had the chance to pull off a few rose petals to

*scatter around her body. What was worse was that
he had, in fact, left the whole flaming bunch. Damn!*

I had forty-five minutes to get showered and start
a meal before Fiona arrived. I was beginning to
think that my brilliant idea of inviting her for a meal
was a bad one. I had been delayed at the station by
an irate Bob Archer complaining about his smashed
headlight. Some one had reversed into his parked
car and what was I, me personally, going to do
about it? He had been so belligerent that it was half-
past six when I had left. Tonight was going to be a
disaster.

The warm water massaged my back and I felt
tension drip away. I closed my eyes, relaxed and
heard a knock on my front door. Damn! Grabbing a
towel, I splashed down the hall. The knocking
continued. Swearing under my breath, I pulled the
door open.

"Shepherd!"

"Sorry, Sir." His eyes took in the pink fluffy towel
and I saw a smirk play on his lips for a second
before a look of distress pushed it aside. "We've got
another murder. It's Vera Rington."

"But ... There's a patrol car outside her house all
the time," I spluttered. A cold shiver was running
down my spine, and it wasn't because I was
undressed.

"I don't understand it, Sir. Her husband phoned
five minutes ago. I've alerted the team."

"Give me five minutes."

I hurried back into the bathroom, drying myself
quickly as I went. Within three minutes I was

dressed and sitting in my car. I passed the phone to Shepherd and started the engine.

"Just phone Fiona Davies and explain, will you? Tell her I'll ring her later – but don't tell her who the victim is. I'll let her know myself when I see her."

As I drove through the town, I was hardly aware of Shepherd's voice; my mind was full of questions. How had the killer avoided the patrol? Why hadn't they been suspicious?

Constable Morrison was waiting for us in the drive. I didn't need to say a word, he could see anger written all over my face and he swallowed. His Adam's apple jerked awkwardly in his throat.

"I can't explain it, Sir," he faltered.

"You had better explain it, Morrison. You were here to protect her. I want to know everything that happened on your shift."

Morrison took a step back and lowered his head.

"At six twenty-five, she drove into the garage; the automatic doors had opened as she had approached. She drove in, the doors closed behind her. It was the same routine as the previous nights. There was nothing different, Sir."

"Except for the small fact that she is dead."

"I'm sorry, Sir."

"Tell that to her husband!" I left him and marched up to the garage which was now standing with its door wide open.

Constable Flowers was standing in front of the crumpled body of Vera Rington. A quick scan of the area told me that there was no blood. Flowers

104

stepped back and allowed me to pass. He couldn't look me in the eye either!

I knelt beside the lifeless body of Vera Rington. A pink ribbon was tight against her neck and I could see scratches gouged into the soft flesh of her throat, as she had tried to tear it away. On the floor beside her was a bunch of yellow roses; a white handkerchief was in her pocket. I turned to Shepherd.

"Have a look around, lad."

Leaving the garage, I waited for Flowers to approach me and give me his version of events.

"She went into the garage as normal, Sir." He looked at me with fear in his eyes. "She waved to us as she pulled into the drive."

"What time did her husband arrive?"

"About five minutes after she did. He parked in the drive and went into the house through the front door. Then he came running out, shouting."

"How do you know that he didn't kill her himself?" I raised my eyebrows to form a question mark. Flowers' face contorted in concentration. I could see different scenarios flashing in front of his eyes.

"She was killed in the garage, Sir, just as she got out of the car. He would have killed her in the house, surely."

"Perhaps."

"She never even had chance to close the car door, Sir."

"If she was killed in the garage, then the killer must have been in the garage waiting for her."

"We saw no one, Sir."

"Think, Constable. Has anyone visited the house today?"

"A chap came to read the meter in the garage at about five o'clock."

"Did you see him leave again?"

"Yes. I'm sure I saw him leave."

"How did he get into the garage?"

"He must have had a remote or something, the doors opened easily enough."

"What did he look like?"

"Blue suit and a clipboard. Ordinary."

"Hair."

"Dark, I think. Or it might have been blond."

"Glasses?"

"I don't know. Maybe. I didn't take a lot of notice; he was just reading the meter."

"Exactly, lad! He was just reading the meter. That was what he wanted you to think. He wanted you to take absolutely no notice of him whatsoever, and you didn't!"

I headed back to my car leaving Flowers open-mouthed. Passing Morrison, I asked him the same questions and received the same replies.

The church clock chimed eight as Shepherd and I put the last piece of information on the crime-board.

"He's a very clever man," I observed sadly. "He became someone that nobody notices and was able to walk straight in and out."

"There were no fingerprints on the door where he forced it, Sir." Shepherd was checking his notebook.

"I didn't expect there would be."

"What about the button that I found in Vera's hand, Sir. She would have pulled it off when she was struggling. That's a clue."

"That jacket will already be in a bin."

"Sir, you're being pessimistic – it's a clue."

"No it isn't!" I shouted at him and watched his face whiten in shock as my frustration lashed out at him. "It's worthless! We have two dead women. We have nothing to connect them. We don't have any motive for either murder. We haven't got a thing. We are, lad, in a very dark place from which there is no chance of escape. Welcome to Copper's Hell, lad. This is where you spend your time running around in circles while the bodies pile up." I slammed my desk drawer shut and left the office. Shepherd didn't move.

Taking a deep breath, I knocked on Fiona's door. When it opened, I was welcomed with a hug and a kiss.

"Have you eaten? I can rustle up some pasta, if you like?"

She took my hand and led me towards the kitchen. Regaining control, I led her towards the lounge where I sat her down. The sofa purred as I sat down beside her and I took both of her hands in mine. "Fi, I'm so sorry."

Her face lost its brightness and I saw concern sitting on her shoulder, watching me. "The call I had, Fi, it was about Vera. She's been murdered."

She pulled her hands from mine and covered her face, forcing back the scream of horror that I had heard starting to rush out from her lungs. "I only said goodbye to her a couple of hours ago. Oh, Mike! Why, Vera?"

"I wish I knew. I'm pretty sure that it's the same man who murdered Suzanne Lloyd. I can't think of anything at all to connect them. I have no idea why either of them is dead."

"Vera would probably have known her; as a doctor's receptionist, Vera would know pretty much everybody. But that's it. Poor Gerald, How is he?"

"You can imagine. When I left, the son had just arrived."

Fiona looked down and I watched her hands pulling imaginary threads from her jeans.

"How did…"

"She was strangled."

"Poor Vera!" She turned to me, laid her head on my shoulder and wept.

As I unlocked the car to go back to my cottage, I heard someone call my name. Martin Goddard was approaching me, wheeling his bike; his glasses reflected the street lights and made it look as if he were some sort of alien invader.

"Out a bit late, aren't you, Mike? Don't the police ever sleep?"

"This policeman will be sleeping as soon as I can get home." I looked at his bike and his lycra exercise shorts. "Still exercising, Martin?"

"Fitness is everything, Mike." He came closer and leaned in conspiratorially. "Is everything ok with the good doctor? She's not committed a crime, has she?" He laughed and I felt the hairs on the back of my neck bristle with annoyance. I still hadn't forgotten how upset Fiona had been when we had bumped into him the other evening.

"Just delivering some bad news. You'll hear about it yourself in due course."

"You mean Vera? Yes, terrible business."

I looked at him open-mouthed. God, the town grapevine had certainly lost no time in broadcasting tonight's headlines.

"I'll see you around, Mike. Remember that we still have a badminton game to arrange." With a quick wave, he was on his bike and cycling into the distance before I had a chance to reply. Never mind, he would soon find out that Richard and I were joining a non-participation group, and he wasn't invited!

Looking back at the house, I saw that the downstairs lights had been extinguished. Fiona was on her way to bed. I yawned. My bed was calling and Ophelia would be pacing the hall, anxious for my return.

Twenty One

The crime-board was beginning to look like a canvas by Jackson Pollock; there were splodges everywhere with nothing to connect them. To me, it was worthless, but to an art dealer it would probably be a masterpiece and worth a small fortune. As far as art was concerned, I preferred nice, clean straight lines; things I could understand like Van Gogh's 'Sunflowers'. Today's modern stuff left me cold, and that was what I was feeling now. Icy fingers of fear were creeping into my mind. I was beginning to be afraid that I would never solve this case and that more blood would be spilt.

Sitting down, I examined the button that Shepherd had found yesterday. It was just a perfectly ordinary button. I looked at my own jacket sleeve. My buttons were identical to this one. Maybe I was the murderer! Maybe I should just arrest myself! This case was starting to play with my mind.

Sighing, I picked up my pen, pulled the blotter towards me, emptied my mind and scribbled. Sometimes the subconscious can work miracles. Perhaps my doodles would find links that I didn't know I had.

A knock at the door interrupted me and I threw down the pen as Shepherd came in with a mug of tea and two custard creams. I glanced down at the mess that I had made of my blotter; what a waste of time and ink.

"Did you find the statements from Morrison and Flowers on your desk, Sir?"

I nodded while I pulled a custard cream apart and

110

ate the half without the cream first; I always saved the best till last. It was as I was studying the pale yellow cream that a thought came crashing into my brain, scattering all of the dozing thoughts like a bowling ball hitting the pins.

"Yellow roses?"

"Sir?"

"We have found yellow roses at every scene. Agreed?"

"Yes. Petals were scattered around the pigs and Suzanne Lloyd had rose petals in her pocket."

"Exactly! He's made his first mistake."

"Who?"

"Think, lad. What didn't we find in Vera's garage?"

"Petals, Sir."

"But what did we find?"

Shepherd looked at me and I could see confused thoughts jumping over the frown lines on his forehead. "A button?"

"And a bunch of yellow roses!"

"But they were Vera's, she bought them home with her."

"Did she? Are you sure?"

"Morrison and Flowers didn't see anyone carrying flowers."

"Morrison and Flowers didn't see a lot. They saw what the killer wanted them to see – an official with a clipboard. They can't even say for sure what colour hair he had. Phone the local florists. See how many bunches of yellow roses were sold yesterday and who to."

Shepherd left the room and I reached for the

second custard cream. Alone once again, I had a closer look at the doodles on my blotter. There, in the centre of the pad was a circle of roses. Why?

By lunchtime, all our enquiries had drawn blanks. House to house calls revealed nothing of note; some people might have a seen a man reading meters while others saw nothing. As for the florists, only 'Tulips' recalled selling a bunch of roses. Unfortunately, it had been a mixed bunch and not totally yellow. I locked my drawer and left the office. I needed some fresh air.

As I was reaching for the station door-handle, Shepherd came bounding up behind me,

"Steady, lad. Where's the fire?"

"Gosberton, Sir."

"There's a fire in Gosberton?"

"No, Sir."

"So where is the fire?"

"There isn't one. I decided to phone the out of town florists and 'Flowers 4 You' was asked to make up a bunch of yellow roses yesterday afternoon."

"Good work! And?"

"The assistant didn't recognise the man but she thinks he was wearing a suit and she's pretty sure that he had dark hair and glasses. He paid cash."

"It's definitely a possible sighting. A suit would suggest that he works in an office. What about his age?"

"She thinks early forties."

"Anything else?"

"He got into a big silver car that was parked

outside the shop."

"Fantastic. We might actually have something to work with now. What about make of car?"

"No idea, she just said it was big."

"Well, let's be positive. At least we know that we are not looking for a silver mini. I feel like celebrating, lad. Are you coming?"

The King's Head was quiet. It was not yet one o'clock, so we got our drinks and settled ourselves in the corner. The news of the silver car had awakened my appetite and my stomach was purring as it waited to receive the cod and chips that I had just ordered. Shepherd had opted for a ploughman's lunch.

"So, lad, do you know anyone who drives a big silver car?"

"No one of my age, Sir. We all tend to drive a 306."

"True." I recalled Shepherd's dark red car in the station car park. I decided to change the subject. "So, when are you and Cat off to London?"

"At the end of the month, Sir, I have some holiday leave due. Did I tell you that we have booked to see a show as well?"

I shook my head.

"Cat wanted to see 'Mother Goose' or some other random nursery rhyme, but I told her it's the wrong time of year for pantomimes. I've persuaded her to see 'Phantom of the Opera.' Have you seen it, Sir?"

"No, but I've heard it's excellent. Whenever I take a trip to the theatre, I always tend to go to Stratford-upon-Avon. I'm sure that Cat will love it."

"It'll be much better than a pantomime."

"The last panto that I saw was 'Jack and the Beanstalk'. I went with …" I stopped and Shepherd looked up at me. "Nursery rhymes!"

"Sir?"

"You said nursery rhymes. Which is the one about the roses?"

"'Roses are red, violets are blue'."

"No!" I closed my eyes and pictured the doodle on my pad. A ring of roses! "Got it! 'Ring-a-ring of roses, a pocket full of posies. Atishoo! Atishoo! We all fall down'"

"Well done, Sir." Shepherd picked up his pint.

"Think about it, lad, he keeps leaving roses – a ring of roses around the pigs and Suzanne had a pocketful of roses."

"But what else fits with the rhyme, Sir? There isn't anything."

"True but …" Frank arrived with our lunches and all conversation stopped. However, I was still convinced that the answer lay in the nursery rhyme. I just had to find out how.

The door of the pub opened and I saw Martin Goddard walk in with a chap that I didn't know, but who seemed very familiar. Martin wasn't looking his normal ebullient self and I breathed a sigh of relief. I didn't exactly want one of his usual lectures about fitness and exercise while I had a mouthful of chips. I caught his eye, and was surprised to see him hesitate before he came over. He didn't seem pleased to see me.

"Martin, how are you?" I half stood to greet him and was once again taken by surprise; he made no attempt to shake my outstretched hand. His companion, however, seized it and pumped it violently. I stumbled through an introduction

"Detective Inspector Mike Malone, pleased to meet you."

"Jeff Goddard, Martin's kid brother. So you're the local copper?"

I sat down again. That was why he had seemed familiar; the family resemblance was pretty obvious and I had missed it. Some police officer I was! Jeff leaned amicably over the table while Martin stood in the shadows. Something was evidently not well in the Goddard family. My guess was that Jeff was the more successful of the two brothers and poor old Martin was bristling with jealousy. He didn't look in my direction the whole time; his gaze was drilling holes in the back of his brother's head.

"Just popped over to finalise details with Martin about next weekend." Jeff was cheerful and talkative, too talkative, as I could see Martin wishing that he would keep family business in the family. "Did Martin tell you that he's going to be a godfather to my little girl?"

"No, he hadn't mentioned it." A sideways glance at Martin showed me that his lips were now even tighter.

"Yes, Alicia's now nearly two months old." He pulled his wallet out from his jacket and thrust a picture of a sleeping baby under my nose.

"Lovely, congratulations," but I wasn't really taking a lot of notice. It was Martin that had all of my attention. There were so many emotions washing over his face that I was feeling sea-sick. He seemed to be horrified rather than pleased.

"Anyway, enjoy your meal." Jeff was gone and as the whirlwind died down, I had a feeling that something very significant had just occurred.

"God, that's a bit insensitive," Shepherd whispered, leaning over so that he wasn't overheard.

"What?" I was still watching the Goddard brothers. Martin was dragging along behind Jeff in the manner of a very sulky child; his head was down and he looked defeated.

"Did you know that Martin Goddard had a daughter who died?"

I nodded, recalling my conversation with Richard yesterday lunchtime when he had told me Martin's life story. "Yes I had heard something."

"Well, her name was Alicia. So why on earth would his brother call his daughter, Alicia? Surely he must realise that it would upset Martin?"

"That's families for you!"

I put down my knife and fork and pushed my plate away. My appetite had disappeared and had been replaced by a sharp pain in my mind. A piece of information that I had come across today was stabbing me mercilessly, trying to get my attention. I sighed and watched Shepherd finish his lunch.

"Ready, lad? I need to revisit everything that we have done today. Something important has happened. I don't know what it is, but I have a feeling that it will take us one step closer to catching our killer."

Following Shepherd out of the pub, we walked across the car-park to find my Mondeo. As we turned the corner, we both stopped and looked at each other. Parked next to my battered green Mondeo was a shiny, silver-grey Mercedes.

Twenty Two

I heard Shepherd put the phone down. A second later and he poked his head around the corner of my door.

"Well, lad? Who does it belong to?"

"Martin Goddard, Sir."

"He must have bought it recently. He was driving a BMW when Fiona and I saw him a couple of days ago. See if you can find out whether anyone else in the area has a big silver car – don't just stick to Mercedes, look for other types as well."

"Yes, Sir." He closed my door and silence closed in on me, waiting. Getting up from my seat, I went and stood in front of the crime-board. Martin Goddard? Should I be arresting him because he's got a silver car? No, the idea was preposterous. There were thousands of silver cars out there.

I kept returning to the nursery rhyme. 'Ring-a-ring of roses.' I was convinced that the missing link was in that rhyme, but as Shepherd was at pains to point out, the only connection between the rhyme and the crimes was roses.

I studied the identikit photo. Short, dark curly hair, glasses, a jacket with a sleeve button missing, a bike and a silver car. Martin fitted it almost perfectly. But he seemed such a nice guy except ...
I remembered how his coldness towards Fiona had upset her. Why, even today, when his brother was talking about the baby, Martin had shown a sulky side. The baby! Alicia!

Alarm bells were ringing in my head. I could hear the whistle and could see flashing lights. Alicia!

Was she the missing link? But how? What connection was there between a dead girl, dead pigs, a dead teacher and a dead receptionist? I needed more background information. Picking up the phone, I invited the only other member of the non-badminton club for a drink after work.

As I put the phone down, Shepherd poked his head around the door again.

"Guess who has recently bought a silver BMW, Sir?"

"Surprise me!"

"Bob Archer."

"Bob Archer." I rolled the name around my mouth, but it tasted all wrong. For all my dislike of Archer, deep down, I did not believe him capable of these horrible crimes; he was the type to get others to do his dirty work. Added to that, Bob's stomach and a bicycle! That would never have happened! I could safely cross him off my list.

The steaks had been first class and as for the apple crumble and custard! I could feel the waistband of my trousers struggling to find an extra inch of elasticity. I sat back in my chair and picked up my pint. Opposite me, Richard was making sure that he had not missed a single speck of cream, the spoon was going round and round and round his bowl.

"Bloody good meal, Mike!"

"Frank has never let me down yet." I put my glass down, took a deep breath and leaned forward. Richard grinned.

"I knew it! There is never such a thing as a free meal, is there? Everything has a price."

I looked away sheepishly.

"It's alright, Mike. Only joking. Now, what do you want to know? Remember on financial matters, my lips must be well and truly sealed. Client confidentiality and all that."

"Thanks, Richard," I smiled uncomfortably. "What I am actually wanting, between you and me, is background on Martin Goddard."

"Good old Martin! This isn't still about the lovely Dr Davies, is it?"

I didn't look at him and I hoped that my reluctance to do so would convince him that Fiona was still what I was thinking about. After all, I could hardly tell him what I was really thinking, if I was thinking anything, and even I wasn't sure at the moment.

"Tell me about his daughter."

"Alicia? Ok, she was a lovely little kid, full of life and the apple of his eye. It totally destroyed him when she died."

"How?"

"Swine flu! You remember that epidemic – no, you weren't here then, were you? Anyway, the town took a bit of a hit with the bug. Even good old Dr Foreman caught it. That was the first time we all set our eyes and hearts on the lovely doctor and our blood pressures went through the roof. She came as locum while he was ill."

He stopped to loosen his tie and finish his pint. As my glass was empty, I took the opportunity to go to the bar and get two more beers.

"Thanks, Mike. Now where was I? Well, Alicia suffered with asthma and when she caught the bug,

120

she couldn't fight it off. Poor thing died on her birthday."

My thoughts were running in all directions with pieces of the jigsaw in their hands; they were trying to bash them into place. As I wrote the words 'swine flu' and 'birthday' in my notebook of the mind, I had a very good idea what the answer to my next question was going to be.

"How old was Alicia when she died?"

"It was on her eighth birthday."

Bingo! The birthday cakes had eight candles on them. Swine flu was supposed to have originated from swine – I think – but anyway a layman would certainly blame a pig. The dots were being to join.

"I don't expect that he was too chuffed when his brother called his new baby, Alicia, was he?"

"He hasn't mentioned it. It's almost as if he has gone into himself. That brother of his is an unfeeling bastard, he really is. You know when the baby was born, don't you?"

"No idea."

"Only on Alicia's birthday. That kid will forever remind Martin of his loss. His brother's a pillock to push Martin's face in it. Excuse me a mo, Mike, just need the loo!"

Richard left his seat and I mulled over everything that I had learned. I could see how the birth of the baby could have triggered something inside Martin. It would have brought back painful memories and I suppose it could have manifested itself in a desire to wipe all pigs off the face of the earth. No pigs, no swine flu. The fact that the virus was airborne wouldn't even elicit a response. It was called swine flu – the swine had to pay. But how did Suzanne Lloyd and Vera Rington fit into this jigsaw? Why were they killed? Try as I might, I still could not picture the Martin that I knew as a cold blooded murderer.

As Richard came out of the Gents and took his seat again, my thoughts dropped the remaining jigsaw pieces and went off to have another long think.

As I sat in the garden with a cup of coffee, I tried to make sense of all that Richard had told me. A blackbird was singing brightly and Ophelia, rather than stretching out beside me, was busily exploring the part of my garden that I liked to call wild. In actual fact, it was just left untended, but this time of year I always found the collage of different greens and leaves aesthetically pleasing to the eye. Having seen Fiona's immaculately tended borders, I knew that she would be itching to get her hands on my undergrowth. I would actually have to stay firm if I wanted to keep her hands from my wilderness.

I had phoned Shepherd as soon as Richard and I had left the pub, and he was coming round early in the morning so that we could take Martin in for questioning about the attacks on the local pigs. Like me, he couldn't see any link between the pigs, Suzanne Lloyd and Vera Rington.

The sound of the church bells floated in the warm breeze and I stretched out, closed my eyes and allowed myself to be soothed by their music. I felt Ophelia jump onto my lap, evidently fed up with her quest, and put out a hand to stroke her. The evening sun had made her coat warm and soft. I followed the contours of her body and found her velvety ears. From there I ran my finger down towards her nose. My eyes opened with a start. Instead of a warm, damp button of a nose, I had found my fingers caressing two slimy rough legs. A frog! Ophelia was sitting on my knee with a frog hanging out of her mouth! My sharp intake of breath alerted her to the fact that I was not happy with having a frog on my knee and she leapt off in disgust. As she wandered back down to the end of the garden, all I could see were two green legs wriggling out of the side of her mouth.

With the mood now broken, I went back indoors. As I passed through the hall, I noticed that the message light on the phone was flashing. Funny! I hadn't heard it ring, but then I had been concentrating upon the church bells. I pressed it.

"Mike! It's Fiona. Can you come over? Something's happened, I …"

I was in the car before the message had finished.

"Has anything been taken?" I was examining the door that led into the garden. The lock had been forced.

Fiona shook her head. She was sitting at her kitchen table, idly tracing the knots in the wood with her fingertips.

"I'm pretty sure that there's nothing missing. But, Mike, things have been moved around."

"I can fix this door for you tonight, but you need to get a locksmith to come tomorrow."

"Ok." She still wasn't looking at me and her voice

was flat and toneless.

"Fiona!"

"Mm?" She finally raised her eyes and smiled.

"Are you sure that you're ok?"

"Yes I'm … I'm not. It's the thought of everything being touched, looked at. I feel dirty."

"Show me what was moved."

She pushed herself reluctantly to her feet and taking my hand, she led me into the hall where she pointed to the walls.

"For a start," she murmured, "these pictures have been swapped around. They're in the wrong places." We went into the lounge. "Look, the clock has been moved forward by two hours and these pictures have also been swapped around. As for the photos on the fireplace, not only have they been moved but he's swapped the photos within the frames as well. Why would … Oh my God!"

Her hand let go of mine and flew to her face, "There! Look!"

Following the direction of her gaze, I saw the photograph of her graduation, a photograph of a cat and …

"Jesus!"

Kneeling down and using my jacket sleeve, I picked up the simple silver frame. Within it was the photograph of a gravestone with the name 'Fiona Davies' photo-shopped onto it. I slipped into one of the plastic bags that I always keep on me.

"What was in the frame?"

"A photo of Tiffany, my cat – that one." She pointed to a photograph of a tortoiseshell cat perched on a wall.

124

"So, which photograph is missing?"

She looked around her, mentally ticking off the photographs. "One of me wearing my first white doctor's coat. Mike, I'm frightened."

"Someone is playing mind games with you, but I'm not sure why. Do you want me to stay tonight?"

She nodded, drew me closer to her and laid her head on my shoulder. I kissed the top of her head, nuzzling her soft blonde hair.

"Ok. I'll sort things out at the cottage and be back within half an hour."

Twenty Three

*He sat in front of his computer screen, twisting the
key between his fingers. As he deleted the image of
the gravestone, he smiled. The silly cow would be so
freaked out by the displaced pictures that she
wouldn't even notice that the spare key was
missing. He could walk into her house any time he
liked. She would pay for what she had done. He
laughed loudly. In fact, by the time that he had
finished with her, she would be begging him to kill
her.*

I decided to pick Shepherd up on the way to the
station. As he got into the car, he smiled broadly.

"You're smelling very nice this morning, Sir.
Very floral." His eyes grew wider and I felt myself
blushing. "You must tell me what it is; it would
make an excellent present for one of the WPCs." He
laughed as my face became even redder.

"I spent the night at Fiona's, if you must know."

Shepherd sniffed again. "Lilies, isn't it, Sir?"

"I didn't have time to go back to mine to shower.
Ok? If you must know she was broken into last
night and was frightened to stay on her own."

"So, you were giving her police protection, Sir?"

I looked across at him, at his blue eyes creased in
laughter and I thought once again of the photograph
in my pocket. David would also have made fun of
me, had a laugh at my expense.

"Definitely, lad. That's was coppers do, give a bit
of protection when it is needed." His good mood
was infectious and I joined in with the joke.

"I'm glad, Sir. She's a nice lady."

"I know, lad. I know."

I turned into Martin Goddard's drive and parked behind the silver Mercedes. The downstairs curtains were still closed, but I could see that those at the upstairs windows had been pulled back.

"Come on, lad. Let's see what he has to say."

We left the car and walked up to the imposing wooden door. I rang the bell. Inside the house I could hear footsteps coming down the stairs and the sound of shoeless feet padding towards the door. The lock was pulled back and the door opened. I watched carefully as the expression on Martin's face changed from surprised to uneasy to confident. He blinked and smiled.

"Mike, you're a bit early, aren't you? You're lucky to have caught me. I was just going for an early morning run."

"Can we come in, Martin? You know Detective Sergeant Shepherd, don't you?"

"Yes, of course." He opened the door wider to allow us to follow him into the kitchen. He swept scattered documents into a pile and gestured for us to sit. We remained standing.

"Coffee?"

He had the kettle in his hand.

"Actually, Martin, we would like you to accompany us to the station. There are some questions that we would like to ask you."

His eyes widened, but in my opinion, the surprise that he was showing was all an act.

"Sounds intriguing! What questions, Mike? Am I a suspect in a crime? How wonderful!"

He had the look of an excited child, I was almost expecting him to clap his hands and jump for joy.

"We'll discuss it at the station. Would you mind if we had a look around?"

Instantly, his face changed. The childish exuberance was replaced by an almost cold savagery.

"You do have a search warrant, don't you?"

"I didn't think that you would mind. After all, you have nothing to hide, do you, Martin?"

"When, and only when I see a search warrant, will I allow you to have a look around. Shall we go?"

Shepherd raised his eyebrows and I shook my head and turned to Martin.

"After you, Mr Goddard."

"Tuesday the fourteenth of June. Seven fifty-five am. Present are Detective Inspector Malone, Detective Sergeant Shepherd and Mr Martin Goddard." I nodded at Martin. "Would you confirm your identity, please, Mr Goddard?"

"Martin Goddard."

"Pigs, Mr Goddard. What do you have against pigs?"

Martin's face was still, there was not a flicker of emotion.

"Why should I have anything against pigs? What a strange question."

He folded his hands in front of him, his eyes never once straying from mine.

"Swine flu, Mr Goddard. I believe that it was swine flu that killed your daughter?"

His eyes narrowed and for a split second, it was

difficult to recognise the amiable chap that I had played badminton with a few days ago.

"Leave Alicia alone!"

"I'll ask the question again, Mr Goddard. What do you have against pigs? Do you hate them because you believe that they are, in some way, responsible for your daughter's death?"

He unclasped his hands, stretched out his fingers and studied them.

"Am I under arrest, Mike?"

"At the moment, you are assisting us in our enquiries."

"So, I'm free to go?"

"As I said, you are helping us with our enquiries. Several pigs in the …"

"So you can't keep me here?" He smiled. "I've got a job to go to. Good-bye, Mr Malone."

He pushed his chair back, making its legs squeal across the floor. He walked purposefully to the door and turned towards me, smiling. He opened the interview room door and I heard his footsteps disappear into the distance.

"Interview terminated at ten minutes past eight."

"What now, Sir?"

"We'll get our search warrant and nail him. He killed those pigs – I can feel it. But I need proof!"

"What about the murders?"

"You saw his reaction to the questions. What do you think?"

"He's certainly cold enough. But what's the motive?"

"Revenge, lad. Revenge."

Twenty Four

If he hurried, he might catch her before morning surgery. Damn him!

He had ruined what was going to be a perfect day.

Sitting at my desk, I contemplated the drawings on my blotter. There were scattered roses and cakes which I expected to see. However, amongst them, there were several handkerchiefs and I had no idea why I had drawn them. I could only assume that my subconscious had put them there for a very good reason. Shepherd arrived with a mug of tea.

"Custard cream?"

"None left, Sir. I've brought two bourbons instead." He looked uncomfortable.

"How do you expect me to think without a custard cream? Go and buy some more."

"But ... yes, Sir."

I could tell by the glance that he threw at me as he shut the door that he was not pleased at being given such a silly errand. I would apologise later, but now I had other things on my mind. I scribbled away, drawing new images. I drew lines and circles between them, around them. I excluded some pictures and included others. The handkerchiefs fluttered underneath my pen as the vast sweeps of my strokes disturbed them. I watched them float from one side of the pad to the other. Frantically, I drew more and more circles, trying to capture them, to force them to stay still so that I could think. Suddenly, my pen caught in the lace edging of a particularly delicate silk hankie and it crumpled. It lay on the centre of the pad as if discarded. One by one the other handkerchiefs fluttered over to join in it and within seconds, I had a pile of crumpled hankies in the centre of the pad surrounded by roses. As the movement on the pad ceased, so the activity in my brain increased. Thoughts appeared from no where, rushing around and opening drawers. With so many drawers and files opening and closing, my head was soon ringing. I squeezed my eyes shut, willing the thoughts to finish their deliberations and come to a conclusion. Silence! As I opened my eyes the answer flashed into my subconscious and I smiled.

When Shepherd opened the door again, his face expressed delight at seeing me, once again, calm and collected.

"You look happy, Sir." He put two custard creams on the plate in front of me and I picked one up and studied it carefully. "The answer, lad, lies with Alicia. We need to find out more about how she died."

"But we know that she died of swine flu, don't we?" He frowned, puzzled.

"Yes we do, but there must be something more that we do not know." I pointed to the crumpled handkerchiefs. 'Atishoo! Atishoo! We all fall down.' Think about the nursery rhyme, lad. Think about the nursery rhyme."

I picked up the second biscuit and dunked it in my tea while Shepherd examined my blotter, trying to make sense of the drawings. I could tell that, as yet, he wasn't entirely convinced.

"Ring the hospital and find out the events

surrounding Alicia's death, lad. See what you can find out."

"Yes, Sir."

He left the office. As I finished the last of my tea, I swept up the blotter, and all of the hankies, and dropped them in the bin.

Twenty Five

He let himself into the house. Going from room to room, he was amused to notice that she had swapped back all of the photographs. He looked at his watch and saw that there was still half an hour before morning surgery finished. If she had calls to make, she might be back by one thirty. Two and a half hours to kill. Two and a half hours to get everything ready. Plenty of time. He went into the kitchen and switched the kettle on. There was even time for a cup of tea.

I tapped out numbers on a calculator. The Chief Constable wanted the overtime figures for the previous quarter and I was three days late. He had already been on the phone complaining. Didn't he know that I had two murders to solve? Shepherd knocked and poked his head around the door.

"I've got the search warrant for Martin Goddard's, Sir."

"Good, we'll call on him now and he can give us a guided tour of his lovely home."

"I also spoke to Records at the hospital, Sir. Alicia died as a result of complications brought about because she was asthmatic."

"Ok. Anything else?"

"The doctor who signed the death certificate is on morning rounds at the moment. She will call me as soon as she finishes."

"When?"

"About two."

I checked my watch. Twelve forty-five. "Right,

that gives us plenty of time to visit Mr Goddard. Come on, lad."

I pulled up outside the local department store. The windows were full of mannequins in bright, tropical attire. I looked down at my boring, grey suit. Hawaiian shirt and shorts perhaps? No, the world was not ready! Baker Goddard was on the corner about ten metres in front of us. Looking around, I couldn't see Goddard's silver Mercedes and I wondered whereabouts he parked it.

The door opened into a bright reception area. A young woman with jet black hair and dark menacing eyeliner looked up from her computer screen. Instinctively, I raised my hand to protect my throat, convinced that I would see fangs as soon as she opened her mouth to speak. With my free hand, I located my ID card which I offered to her.

"Detective Inspector Malone and Detective Sergeant Shepherd. We'd like to see Martin Goddard."

As she handed the ID card back, I saw her blood red fingernails and was even more concerned for my safety.

"Mr Goddard phoned in sick this morning." I was surprised that her voice was so gentle and pleasant. I smiled at her and lowered my hand.

"Thank you, we'll catch him at home." I wondered what he was trying to hide that had stopped him going into work. Silently, I cursed my lack of foresight in not going armed with a search warrant earlier.

Shepherd opened the door and I followed him out

134

onto the street.

"Now that, lad, was definitely Morticia Addams."

"No, Sir. Her name was Lisa, it was on her name badge."

I rolled my eyes. Did the youth of today know nothing?

Fifteen minutes later we pulled up outside Goddard's home.

"The car's not here, Sir."

"It might be in the garage, lad. Go and ring the bell."

Shepherd walked over to the front door while I tried the garage door. It was unlocked!

"No reply, Sir. I'll try round the back."

His receding footsteps were drowned out by the sound of the garage door sliding upwards.

Inside the garage, there were boxes everywhere. There wouldn't even have been room for a bike. When Shepherd joined me, I had already opened the first box.

"Sir? Should we?"

"We do have a search warrant, lad, or had you forgotten?"

He grinned sheepishly and kneeling down, he opened a second box.

"I've got lots of children's books and toys here, Sir. They're all Alicia's, I expect."

"So far, I've got old files, accountancy books and dusty ledgers."

"School books, as well, Sir."

I could hear him flicking through the books while I scanned page after page of figures.

"Sir?"

His tone of voice told me immediately that he had found something.

"Sir, Alicia's teacher was Suzanne Lloyd."

I put down my pile of files and examined the faded blue exercise book that he had passed over. On the front cover, written in a childish script, was 'Alicia Goddard. Y3. Mrs Lloyd.'

"Well done. This proves that Goddard knew her. But I'm still not seeing a motive for murder here." I was still fumbling, still trying to make connections. I kept returning to the Martin Goddard that I knew; he did not come across as the type of chap who could coldly slit another human being's throat. And, why on earth would he want to kill his daughter's teacher anyway?

Shepherd was still busily pulling books and toys from his box and I watched him. He was always so careful, so industrious, so conscientious.

"Look at this, Sir." He held out a large sketch pad. "It looks as if Alicia liked to draw pigs."

I took the book from him and opened it randomly. A large, pink, porcine face stared back at me. I turned the page; even more pigs. Alicia had even given them names.

"His daughter liked pigs and he blamed them for her death." I put the book down. "Come on, lad. I want to see what he threw away after we left this morning."

We stacked the boxes away again and left the garage, pulling the door down behind us. Shepherd led the way to the back of the house and pointed to a black bin bag which had been all neatly tied up and was awaiting collection. Pulling out a pair of gloves, I dropped to my knees and carefully untied the knot. The smell of rotting food hit me, but nevertheless, I thrust my hand in deeply. Shepherd held the mouth of the bag open so that we could have more light.

Tea bags, lots of tea bags and ready-meal cartons. I noticed with a smile that unlike me, Goddard chose the low calorie versions. I found a pile of soggy letters, but they fell apart as soon as I touched them.

"Any luck, sir?"

"It would have been nice to find a box of rat poison, wouldn't it?"

I carried on sifting through the waste products of Martin Goddard's life, but all to no avail. I was just about to give up when the corner of a box in the bottom of the bag caught my eye. Moving aside the remains of something that I took to be sweet and sour chicken, I pulled out a box that in its past life had held sixteen pink birthday candles. I presented it to Shepherd who dropped it into a plastic bag.

"It might not be poison, but it'll do nicely."

I retied the bag and turned my gloves inside out so that they wouldn't stain my jacket.

"Right, let's get back to the station and send out an alert. Let's see where the 'sick' Mr Goddard has got to today."

Twenty Six

Hearing the car on the gravel drive, he checked his watch. Twenty-five to two. She was late! Putting his cup in the sink, he opened the door to the utility room and crouched down below the glass in the door. From his hiding place, he heard the key scratching in the lock. The front door opened and closed. Footsteps were getting closer and he recognised the change in sound as the walker moved from carpet to a tiled floor. He saw her head looking out of the window into the garden as she turned on the tap to fill the kettle. When she turned away to plug the kettle in, he made his move. Noiselessly, he opened the utility door and within seconds he was behind her.

"Good afternoon, Dr Davies."

The kettle fell to the floor when he struck her.

With the patrols looking for Goddard's car, we sat in the office waiting for the call from the hospital. I had tried phoning Fiona to see if she wanted to meet for a drink after work, but her mobile was switched off. I checked my watch; quarter to two, she would still be finishing her morning calls.

Shepherd's phone rang and he got up to answer it, leaving me to consider all I knew about Martin Goddard, which wasn't a lot. I decided to give Richard a call.

"Mike! Nice to hear from you, but I don't expect that this is a social call, is it?"

"Sorry, Richard, but you're the only one that I can ask."

"Fire away."

"Thanks." I took a deep breath. "What can you tell me about the circumstances surrounding Alicia's death?"

"Swine flu – I told you."

"I know, but what else can you remember? How long was she ill, that sort of thing?"

"It's a couple of years ago, but I do remember old Martin getting into a right state."

"About what?" My pen was poised to take notes.

"The school."

"The school? Why?"

"Well, Alicia started feeling ill at school, but they didn't send her home. The teacher had thought that Alicia was faking because she didn't want to do a test that afternoon. If I remember correctly, Alicia died the same night."

"Can you remember the name of the teacher?" I asked, although I was pretty sure that I already knew the answer.

"Mrs Lloyd, the one who was mur … Mike! You're not thinking that … are you?"

"I'm not sure, Richard." I sighed deeply. "I'm hoping that I am horribly

wrong. Unfortunately, Martin seems to have gone missing. Do you know where he might have gone?"

"Car or bike?"

"His car's missing."

"Then, sorry, no idea. If he was on his bike, well, I know everyone of his favoured routes; he bores me with them every time we meet."

"Thanks for your help, Richard, and look, at the moment this is between us. Is that ok?"

"No problem. Martin? God, I'd hate to have your job."

"Days like today, I hate to have my job too."

I put the phone down and looked at my blotter. While I had been on the phone, I had put the name 'Martin' behind a prison door.

He sat on the edge of the bath, watching her. There was blood on her head from where she had hit her head as she had fallen. He had felt nothing as he had undressed her; the sight of her naked body had left him cold. There were no feelings of desire, only feelings of hatred. He looked around, everything was ready.

She stirred and he watched the terror rush to fill her eyes as she realised where she was; as she realised that her hands and feet were bound with tape. On any other occasion, the sight of her struggling to hide her nakedness would have amused him. Today he felt only anger as she twisted and turned in the empty bath. The tape across her mouth stopped her from begging for mercy.

He sat and watched her until eventually, exhausted and defeated, she looked at him, pleading for her life. His anger grew fiercer.

"Alicia died gasping for breath and burning with fever. Do you know what it feels like to burn up, Dr Davies? Do you know what it feels like to fight for breath?"

She shook her head and he saw tears. His anger grew fiercer.

"You are going to experience it, Dr Davies. You are going to experience it all before you die."

140

Frantically, she kicked her feet. His anger grew fiercer.

Shepherd came back into the office with his note pad.

"Well, lad?"

The doctor said that there was pretty much nothing they could do."

"Why?"

"If Alicia had been brought in earlier, then medication might have helped. But the local GP had failed to react to the possibility of complications arising because of the asthma and had just prescribed paracetamol and rest."

"The local GP?" I saw Shepherd shuffle his feet in embarrassment and his face redden in discomfort. He lowered his head, studying his notebook carefully. "It was Fiona, wasn't it?"

"Sorry, Sir."

That explained why Goddard had been so cold towards her when we had bumped into him; he blamed Fiona for Alicia's death. But where did Vera Rington fit in? I looked at my watch. Five past two. She would be …

"Her phone was switched off!"

"Sir?"

"Fiona's phone was switched off." I pushed my seat back. My heart was trying to break out of my chest. "She's a doctor, she never has her phone switched off. Come on, lad!"

I pushed past Shepherd, fumbling for my car keys as I ran down the corridor. I heard Shepherd scampering behind me.

"Let me get to her in time," I prayed. "Please let her be safe."

Twenty Seven

He stood over her with the freshly boiled kettle in his hand and enjoyed seeing the panic in her eyes.

"Alicia's skin was burning with fever," he whispered.

He felt no pity for this woman who had destroyed his life. He wanted her to suffer as his daughter had suffered.

"Ready?"

He tipped the kettle. Boiling water fell in a silver stream onto her stomach. He heard her scream trapped behind the tape and watched as she twisted and turned trying to escape. The pale soft skin of her stomach was becoming scarlet and blistered. Violent red snail trails were running in all directions from her stomach, across her hips and down her thighs. She was in agony but he felt no pity. Turning away from her, he left to refill the kettle.

I turned the car into the top of Fiona's street.

"Sir! The Mercedes!"

I followed Shepherd's gaze and saw Goddard's silver car nestling between a Ford Focus and a Honda on the roadside. My heart rate increased again and I could feel cold fingers clawing their way down my spine. I pulled sharply into Fiona's driveway, sending gravel spinning in all directions.

He heard the wheels in the gravel before he got to the kitchen and his anger grew fiercer as he realised that now he would not have the chance to prolong her suffering. Going back to the bathroom, he picked up the plastic bag and pulled it over her head, securing it tightly.

"Alicia struggled to breathe, Dr Davies. Enjoy your death."

He turned his back on her and left the bathroom. As he descended the stairs he heard her struggles becoming weaker.

Shepherd and I rushed to the front door. Fiona's car was in front of the garage. The cold fingers were now twisting my stomach; I felt a wave of sickness and I swallowed the bile back. The door was locked.

"Together," I shouted. "After three!"

We charged the door and it shuddered in shock.

"Again! On the count of three!"

This time the door gave way and we fell into the hall. As I regained my balance, I saw Martin Goddard sitting calmly on the bottom of the stairs.

"Afternoon, Mike. Nice day, isn't it?" He smiled at me.

"Handcuff him and call for an ambulance."

I pushed roughly past him.

"Fiona! Fiona!" I took the stairs two at a time. "Fiona!"

I opened the bedroom door. Nothing.

"FIONA!"

Silence was crowding me. She had to be here. I pushed open the bathroom door and my heart stopped. She was lying naked in the bath. Livid red, angry burns covered her lower body, and a plastic bag covered her beautiful face. Tears welled in my eyes. With a single stride I was on my knees beside her. My fingers clawed at the bag, forcing a way in. I ripped it apart. There she was, my beautiful Fiona. With a shaking hand, I felt for a pulse. I couldn't find one. I fumbled around her neck. I couldn't find a pulse. I reached for her hands. Thick silver tape covered her wrists. I daren't move her because of her burns. I didn't know what to do. Panic was enveloping me.

"ALAN!"

Within seconds, Shepherd was at the door and I heard his gasp of shock.

"I don't know what to do," I cried. I was a helpless child once again.

"The ambulance is on its way. Have you checked for a pulse?"

"I can't find one."

"Let me try."

I watched him take control. He found the pulse point immediately.

"She's alive. The pulse is weak, but she's alive, Sir."

"Thank God!" Tears were on my cheek.

"Let's get water on these burns. Turn the cold tap on, Sir."

Following his command, I gently lifted Fiona's head away from the tap and turned it on. Shepherd turned on the shower so that cold water could cool down her burning skin. As the water hit her skin, I saw her body flinch and relax. I returned to her side and gently continued to remove the bag from her head. That done, I stroked her hair to comfort her, to reassure her. I think she tried to smile, but maybe it was my imagination.

"Where's Goddard?"

"Handcuffed in the kitchen, Sir."

"Go downstairs and take him away. Use my car. I don't want to see him." I threw him my car keys. "Did you call the team as well?"

"Yes, Sir."

"Good, I'll go with Fiona in the ambulance. I'll call you when I want picking up."

"Ok, Sir."

Five minutes later, I heard the car reversing out of the drive. Only the sound of the running water broke the silence.

I raised the cup to my lips and put it down again. It was cold; the third cup of tea that I had left standing. Idly, I picked up the same magazine from the waiting room table and flicked through the same pictures without looking at them.

"Mr Malone?" A soft voice was at the door, bringing me back to life. Her smile made her look a lot younger than I guessed she was. "You can have five minutes."

I followed her down to the end of the corridor; she opened a door and stood aside to let me pass.

Fiona was as pale as the sheets on the bed, but she was alive! I touched her hand and she opened her eyes. She smiled.

"You saved my life." Her voice was soft and fragile.

"But I couldn't stop him hurting …" My voice shattered into pieces.

"But you saved my life."

"I'm never going to let anyone hurt you ever again."

"Good." She squeezed my fingers and closed her eyes.

"I'll see you tomorrow." I kissed her forehead and gently removed my hand from hers. She was still smiling when I left the room.

What did the doctors say, Sir?" Shepherd started the car and we made our way out of the labyrinth that was the hospital car-park.

"Third degree burns to her stomach. She's going to need several skin grafts. Otherwise, ok."

"That's good."

"Goddard?"

"In custody. He admitted everything."

"Even Vera Rington?"

"Yes. Vera wouldn't give him an appointment to see the doctor." He pulled up at the traffic lights. "When he tried to make an appointment for Alicia, Vera said that there were none available. Even though he stressed that it was urgent, she told him to ring back the next day."

"Killed because she did her job."

He pulled away as the lights turned green.

"When Goddard called the emergency number later that night, Dr Davies came out. She told him to give Alicia some paracetamol."

"But she got worse."

"Yes. He called an ambulance later that night, but she died in hospital."

"So it was all about revenge. I suppose his brother's baby brought all of the memories of that day flooding back."

"That's right."

He turned into my drive.

"Thanks, lad. Now I'd better run you home."

"Don't be silly, Sir. You look worn out. Anyway, Cat is meeting me here, she wants to know how you are."

"In that case, I suppose I should put the kettle on."

"Sounds like a good idea, Sir."

As I opened the door, Ophelia trotted down the hall to meet me, grumbling because she was hungry. My own stomach rumbled a loud greeting to her and I realised that I hadn't eaten since lunchtime. I saw Shepherd looking at my stomach, smiling.

"I'll get her to bring some chips with her as well, Sir."

Twenty Eight

Even though visiting time wasn't until the afternoon, the duty nurse allowed me to have ten minutes with Fiona. Her face lit up when she saw me brandishing a large bouquet of flowers. I laid them on the bedside cabinet and leaned over to kiss her.

"How are you feeling?"

I pulled a chair up beside the bed and took her hand, stroking her fingers gently.

"Sore. They say that I'll need skin grafts. Oh, Mike," her eyes filled, "I'm going to look such a mess."

"Never! You, Dr Davies, are a little cracker." I raised her hand to my lips. "As I said last night, if you remember, I'm going to look after you. You can even stay with me when you get out, if you don't want to be on your own. I can cook a pretty mean ready-meal!"

She said nothing, just smiled briefly. Her mind was elsewhere, I don't even know if she had heard me.

"Have you got him?"

"Yes."

"He wanted me to die like his daughter. He blamed me!"

"He blamed a lot of people for his daughter's death."

"But I was the only one he wanted to suffer." She turned away from me and tried to pull her hand away. I kept hold of her "Was he responsible for everything, even the pigs?"

"He blamed everyone and everything for Alicia's death. He didn't think that her death was justified and he wanted others to pay for it."

"But that is so wrong. How could anyone do that?"

This time I didn't answer, this time it was me who turned away. I sensed her turn to look at me.

"Mike?"

"My son – David – he was murdered."

"Oh, Mike!" She squeezed my hand tightly and even though I was aware of her fingernails pressing into my skin, I still couldn't look at her.

"My memories of that day are firmly locked away, Fi. They have to be because I know … I know that if they ever got out, I would be looking for revenge, just as Martin Goddard did."

"Mike, you're a good, kind man. You wouldn't do that."

"I think I would, Fi. That's why I never talk about David. I need to be in control."

"How old was he?"

"Fifteen. Please don't ask me anything else."

"I won't ask any more. But, Mike, I do believe that you are a really good man. I do believe that you would do the right thing."

"Let's hope that I am never put to the test. Look, I've got to go, Sister, is beginning to look impatient. I'll see you tonight."

I kissed her good-bye and left without looking back at her; I was frightened by what her expression would tell me. I was frightened that she might be disappointed in me. I was frightened that my honesty might have ruined everything.

As the warm air hit me on the steps of the hospital, I took a deep breath to wake up all of the slumbering thoughts in my mind. They immediately all rushed off and returned wearing bright 'Fiona loves Mike' sweaters. Hoping that they were right, I spun around and rushed back into the hospital. I ran down the corridor and past the startled duty nurse. As I opened the door, Fiona looked up and quickly brushed tears from her cheeks. She smiled and held out her arms.

"We're a team, Mike Malone and don't you forget it."

"Is that what the doctor orders?"

"Definitely"

This time our parting had warmth and affection.

"Now I had better go before Sister chases me out with a bed-pan. Love you."

"Love you too."

Leaving the hospital for the second time, I didn't only see a sky full of sunshine; I saw a sky full of rainbows and pink hearts too.

At the station, Shepherd had already taken down the pictures from the crime-board and had separated them into two piles; people and pigs.

"You look happy this morning, Sir. Is Dr Davies ok?"

"She's fine, lad, she's fine."

"Well, I think that deserves a celebration," He glanced at his watch. "A bacon sandwich, Sir?"

I looked at the photographs on my desk and shook my head,

"No thanks, lad. Just *three* custard creams."

ABOUT THE AUTHOR

Milly Reynolds lives in Lincolnshire with her husband, son and two cats. Until recently Milly was a full-time English teacher, but she has now left the profession to devote time to her writing.

Living in Lincolnshire, Milly loves its flat, endless landscapes and tries to incorporate these into her novels. She also has a passion for all forms of crime fiction which was why she decided to create her own 'hero' – Mike Malone. Rather than wanting to compete with the masters of the genre, she made the decision that Mike Malone would be more off-beat; she wants her novels to have humour in them. She wants to make readers chuckle rather than scream.

Happy Deathday To You is the second in the Mike Malone Mysteries.series

Printed in Great Britain
by Amazon